Penelope

a novel

Penelope Farmer

Margaret K. McElderry Books

Margaret K. McElderry Books
An imprint of Simon & Schuster Children's Publishing Division
1230 Avenue of the Americas
New York, New York 10020

Book design by Angela Carlino
The text of this book is set in Garamond 3

Printed and bound in the United States of America
First Edition
10 9 8 7 6 5 4 3 2 1

Library of Congress Cataloguing-in-Publication Data
Farmer, Penelope, 1939–
Penelope / Penelope Farmer.—1st ed.
p. cm.
Summary: Since being abandoned by her widowered father, Flora
lives with her cousin and struggles with memories of a previous life
in which she was the child Penelope.
ISBN 0-689-80121-1 (hardcover)
[1. Reincarnation—Fiction. 2. Identity—Fiction. 3. Cousins—
Fiction. 4.Friendship—Fiction.] I. Title.
PZ7.F2382Pe 1996
[Fic]—dc20 95-18801
CIP
AC

For Clare Penelope with love

Part One

☾

Chapter One

"Daddy, Daddy," screamed the little girl, pulling at her mother's arm. Then "Papa. Papa." About three years old, she was much too young to appreciate paintings, thought the only other person in the room. An elderly man in a corduroy cap, he could not help looking around to see what the little girl was pointing at. She didn't mean *him*, surely? But the little girl was not pointing at the elderly man. Her finger was outstretched toward one of the paintings; a large one in a gold frame of a man reclining on the grass in what looked like a parkland, surrounded by trees. Dressed in a dun-colored coat and breeches and a broad-brimmed black hat, he was staring dreamily out of the picture toward the little girl. In his hand he held a leather-bound book.

"*Shush*, Flora," the child's mother said. Gold-embroidered boots on her feet, her hair a multitude of little braids threaded with beads, she wasn't wearing a wedding ring and looked much too young to be anybody's mother. Glancing anxiously at the old man, she pulled the child back, abruptly, making her feet clatter on the wooden floor. "Shush, Flora," she repeated. "Don't be so silly. Whatever can you mean? That's not your daddy." But the little girl just went on screaming, her voice louder than ever, "Daddy, Daddy." In a moment, worse still, she began to cry, at the same time continuing to insist, "Daddy, Daddy. Papa, Papa."

Flora remembered nothing of the scene in the Tate Gallery. She had been only three at the time. But her Aunt Jo did not forget. Flora's mother had told Jo the whole story—but then she told Jo most things. Jo was her best friend, as well as the sister of Flora's father, though no one talked about that much. Flora's father was a bad lot, according to Aunt Jo. Flora's mother was all right though. Jo had loved her, she said, almost as much as she now loved Flora. The only problem was, Flora's mother didn't have the sense she was born with, Jo said.

Jo herself had a lot of sense, luckily for Flora. If it hadn't been for Jo, who knows what would have become of either Flora or her mother. Even before Flora's mother showed how little sense she had by getting herself run over and killed by a bus, she and Flora had lived with Jo and her family. It was very kind of Aunt Jo and Uncle Frank to let them stay. In the cramped little house in Hammersmith, in the cramped little street between the big hospital where Flora had been born and the cemetery where her mother was buried, there'd scarcely been room for one family, let alone two. Flora and her mother had had to sleep in the front room downstairs, on a sofabed and a camp bed. Their possessions had stood all around them in supermarket bags and boxes. The boxes held books mostly. But in one box, there was a picture, too, wrapped in brown paper and Scotch tape. Flora remembered her mother showing her the picture once. Sometimes she wondered what had happened to it, after her mother died, after Aunt Jo and Uncle Frank had adopted Flora and become her mum and dad.

For a while after that Jo and Frank had moved Flora's camp bed into their own bedroom with them. But when six months or so had passed, Frank said to Flora, "Time you had a proper bed, Florakins." (He was the only person who ever called Flora "Florakins." From him she didn't mind a bit.) And then, for the next six months, he took more time off from his boys' club and his political party committees than he'd done at any other time before or since. Huffing and puffing rather—he was a short, fat man—he built on a bathroom behind the kitchen. And when he'd done that he'd turned the old bathroom upstairs into a bedroom for Flora's cousin Alan. From that time on Flora shared the other bedroom with her cousin Louise, Alan's sister. Even after Alan went away to college she and Louise continued to share it.

Up till the age of ten or so, Flora did not mind having the same bedroom as Louise. Nor did Louise seem to mind sharing it with Flora. The two were more like sisters than cousins. Almost exactly the same age, not unalike to look at, they even dressed alike sometimes.

They'd been mistaken for twins a time or two. Sometimes they pretended they were twins. Secretly Flora wished they really were. She was hurt when Louise said she was glad they weren't. Not that she ever admitted she felt hurt. But then, right from the beginning, Flora always did prefer to keep her feelings to herself. And that, maybe, was one of the problems.

☾

Chapter
Two

Though Flora's calling the man in the Tate Gallery "Papa" was the first time she behaved in such a surprising way, it wasn't the last. As a little girl she kept saying peculiar things—things other people found peculiar, that is. For what she said didn't seem the least bit peculiar to her. She just talked about things she remembered from long ago. And didn't everyone have things they remembered from long ago? There was a little white dog, for instance, with a curly tail, that she remembered loving more than anything in the world. It was true they had no dog at Cardew Road, only a not-very-friendly tabby cat. But that didn't mean to say, she thought, that she hadn't had a little white dog when she was little, before she and her mother had come to live with Aunt Jo and Uncle Frank.

During one Sunday lunch, when she was six or so, she started thinking about the little dog for some reason. And suddenly she remembered that it had died. She could not quite remember how it had died, only that something horrible had happened. She put down her knife and fork and, staring at her plate of roast lamb and green peas, heard herself saying, sadly, "I cried when my dog died. I cried and cried and cried."

Louise laughed at her. "Flora's making up stories," she said. "Flora's always making up stories. We haven't got a dog in our house. We've only ever had a cat."

"But I did have a dog," Flora insisted. "I did have one. It died, I tell you."

Alan was kinder than Louise. "But Flora," he said, leaning forward, "you don't even like dogs. You're frightened of them. Whenever you see a dog you want to run away."

"I'm only frightened of big dogs," Flora protested. "I'm not frightened of little dogs at all."

"Of course you're not," said Uncle Frank, soothingly. He was always particularly kind to Flora. Too kind sometimes, Aunt Jo said. She thought Uncle Frank spoiled both his girls—when he had time to, that is, between his committees. "It makes sense to be frightened of big dogs," he added, smiling at Flora. "Don't let me catch you patting rottweilers, Louise, either."

Flora shuddered. Ever since she was a baby, the sight of any dog bigger than a Labrador had made her start to cry. She had loved the little white dog, though; its name was Tray, she remembered, as she picked up her fork, ready to start eating her dinner again. It died, she thought again. And, as she did so, words came into her head from nowhere, words so loud and so insistent she found herself suddenly repeating them out loud—"Eat or be eaten," she proclaimed, stabbing at a roast potato. "Eat or be eaten." She could not imagine why all of them—Aunt Jo, Uncle Frank, her cousins, Louise and Alan—were staring at her in such amazement. "Eat or be eaten," she repeated for the third time, putting the potato into her mouth and chomping it up.

"Does Flora think a potato could eat *her?*" Louise said.

And then there was this, on a hot day, a year or so later, when Flora and Louise were out shopping with Aunt Jo, in the big supermarket in King's Mall. Seeing a fat man pushing a cart down the aisle just ahead of them, Flora stopped dead, burst out laughing, and said, "He's almost as fat as Doctor Darwin. Only he doesn't have a wig like Doctor Darwin. Do you suppose he believes in God?"

"Who's Doctor Darwin? What's a wig?" Louise asked. "What do you mean, 'believes in God'?" But by then Flora couldn't remember who Doctor Darwin was, either. She stood blinking, staring at the fat man's bald head and round red face, at his nose beaded with sweat where his spectacles touched them. Aunt Jo, very sharply for her, said, "Stop staring, Flora, it's rude. Has the cat got your manners?" At which Louise sniggered, and Flora, furiously, kicked Louise, and Aunt Jo took them by an arm each and dragged them crossly away into the next aisle. And once again, for the moment, as far as Flora and Louise were concerned, that was that.

Aunt Jo remembered the name Doctor Darwin,

though. She wondered if he'd been famous; whether it would be worth looking his name up in the library. But she never did. And gradually, as she grew older, Flora almost stopped being troubled by such memories. Even when the memories did come, she'd grown wise enough over the years to keep them to herself. Jo assumed that the problem was over and done with. But then, at the age of ten or so, Flora and Louise started falling out. And thereafter the memories began returning to Flora, thick and fast. This time they brought with them voices, voices that were forever whispering names in her head. Her name, was it?—yes—it seemed to belong to her. Yet the name she heard the voices whispering wasn't the name everyone else called her—"Flora." And soon they started driving her crazy altogether.

(

Chapter
Three

No one mistook Louise and Flora for twins by this
time. Louise had started to grow much taller and Flora
had not. Flora was a thin, pale, beaky, and above all small
girl, younger looking than her age, and not the least
interested in clothes, boys, or pop music, the way other
girls in her class at school were. She did not mind being
small, or having different interests from everybody else.
But Louise minded Flora being different, or rather it
upset her that Flora did not seem to mind. Louise was a
big girl now, in more ways than one. She was proud of
being the first girl in her class to have to wear a bra. She
thought Flora should have been envious of her for that.
But Flora did not seem envious in the least. Yet Louise
was deeply envious of something Flora had—and that

Flora took for granted: her more than good, her exceptionally good brain.

Not that Louise was stupid; far from it. She was very good at sports, moreover, much better than Flora. She was the best gymnast in the gym class she went to on Saturday mornings. But she did not have the kind of brain that Flora had. Flora's kind made the head of their primary school insist that Flora should try for a scholarship to the big private girls' school. Louise would have got into the school all right, if Jo and Frank could have afforded to pay for her to go. But there was no way she could have won a scholarship to it—whereas Flora won the top scholarship, easily. Worse still, as far as Louise was concerned, she seemed to take winning the scholarship for granted.

Had it not been for Flora, Louise wouldn't have minded in the least going to the school in Chiswick. But she did mind now. In particular she minded hearing her father make a fuss over Flora. "You'll be our next woman prime minister, Flora, see if you aren't," he said. "I'm proud of you, I really am."

Seeing Louise's face, Aunt Jo herself had more sense than to make too much fuss over Flora. What she could not avoid was taking Flora out to buy the uniform for her new school. All Louise needed for her new school was a skirt and blouse, a sweater, a blazer and a pair of gym shorts. Flora had to have those too. But she needed a great many other things besides. A school hat, for instance—two school hats, in fact, one for winter, one for summer. She needed a school overcoat and a school raincoat. She had to have not only a hockey stick but a tennis racquet. The school had its own sports grounds on the other side of the river, and Flora would be doing some kind of sport almost every day of her school life. She could even choose to row on the river, if she wanted. Uncle Frank taught boys to row in one of his clubs. He said he'd be glad to help Flora to learn.

But Flora wasn't interested in the least. *It's not fair*, Louise thought. At her own school she'd be lucky to get one session of sports a week. She might not have thought anything of this except for her own father offering to teach Flora to row. That was the last straw.

Flora had grown used to Louise glaring at her, making sarcastic remarks. She'd grown used, too, to being called brainy, boring, a bookworm, to seeing Louise and her best friend, Tracy Ann, whispering together, then turning to look at her, giggling. But she didn't much like it, and the less she liked it, the more she was plagued by memories from that mysterious past in which she'd loved a little white dog; the more the voices whispered to her her other name, the name that wasn't Flora. She did not tell anyone about it, of course. She just retired to sit by herself in her bedroom and read her books more avidly than ever.

It was easy to see which side of the bedroom belonged to Louise and which to Flora. On Flora's side everything was tidy. Shelves were crammed with her books. Along the windowsill her china and glass animals stood in pairs. Flora had always liked things to come in pairs; there were two teddy bears, even, sitting on her bed, side by side. In the other half of the room, on Louise's bed, sat only one very big, very pink bear with a blue ribbon around its neck. On the shelves above sat Louise's cassette player, her tapes. On the wall were her posters of Michael Jackson and Kylie Mynogue. (Aunt Jo had made her take Madonna down.) There were clothes strewn all over the floor. Louise was what Jo called a 'mucky pup,' unlike Flora.

Flora and Aunt Jo were reading *Wuthering Heights* together at this time. One afternoon Flora walked into the bedroom, the book under her arm, to find that Louise had almost finished making a line down the middle of the floor with old shoeboxes and discarded Lego bricks from the box under Alan's bed. She glared at her cousin and laid down the last barricade of red, white and blue bricks. Then she got to her feet and said, "That's it then. If you leave anything on my side of the room, I'll throw it away. I'll burn it. Especially a book," she said, pointing at *Wuthering Heights*. "One of your cruddy books."

"If I find anything of yours on my side, I'll wrap it up and send it to Oxfam," Flora said, coolly. But she did not feel cool. She felt unhappier suddenly than she'd felt in her whole life. I can't help getting a scholarship, she thought. It's not my fault. For one moment she so wanted to be friends with Louise again, she found herself wishing that she and Louise were after all going to the same school. But only for a moment. Then she turned her back on her cousin, lay down on her bed, and opening her book, pretended to read.

Louise banged about for a while, taking clothes out of her drawers, and putting them back in again. Having opened the cupboard doors and slammed them shut not once but twice, she put on a tape of Michael Jackson, turned the sound up, turned it down, turned it up again. She reached over for Flora's new hockey stick from the corner in which Flora had stowed it, flourished it, and shouted above Michael Jackson's voice, "Who wants to play hockey anyway, it's a snob game." But it was no good. Flora just went on reading or pretending to read. She didn't even lift her eyes from her book when Louise broke her own new rules, invaded Flora's side of the room and drew the curtains, hoping to make it too dark for Flora to read.

"I'm off," she hissed, leaning right over Flora, putting her face between Flora and her book. "I'm off to Tracy Ann's. You're a boring fart, Flora, that's what you are. You can keep your stupid book."

Turning Michael Jackson up louder than ever she shouted, "And you keep to your side. I mean it," and slammed out.

Flora did not draw the curtains back. She did not even turn down Michael Jackson. She just rolled over on her back, clutched her two teddy bears to her, one to either side, and burst into tears.

Michael Jackson fell silent at last. But by then Flora's head was so full of other voices, she did not notice. They were shouting now, like people shouting at a football game—not that Flora had ever been to a football game, but she had seen them on television, often enough. After a while, a lone voice replaced them, a woman's this time. The woman seemed to be weeping. She was repeating over and over the name the voices had always whispered in Flora's head, her middle name: "Penelope." But in a moment this weeping voice was drowned out by another, still more familiar, rich, gravelly voice. It was shouting, or rather stammering, in triumph, over and over . . . "Eat or be eaten."

Flora clutched her head at this point. It hurt so. EAT OR BE EATEN. She could not bear it. The insistent voice was running the words together now. They came out sounding like one word, making her skull start throbbing and banging away. It felt like someone tying steel bands around her head, pulling them tighter by the minute. It felt like someone else thumping inside her skull with a small but heavy hammer. After a while she began to scream in pain. Almost immediately Aunt Jo came running.

☾

Chapter
Four

That was the first of Flora's bad headaches. They did not last long—not more than five or ten minutes usually. But Jo worried about them all the same. After a week or two she consulted their doctor. The doctor referred Flora to the specialist at Charing Cross Hospital. Despite making many tests, the specialist had been so baffled he'd referred her to yet another doctor, a very nice, gentle woman who did not prod Flora with cold hands, fix electrodes to her head, or give her pills or medicines. Instead she sat her down and asked embarrassing questions about whether there was anything worrying her and so on. Flora refused to answer. If there *was* anything worrying her it was no one's business but her own.

*　*　*

It was September by now. Flora started at her new school. Louise started at hers. For a while then, the headaches abated. Flora was very happy at school at first. It didn't seem to matter that, as usual, she made no friends, for she loved all the new subjects to which she was being introduced; French and Latin, for instance. In history they were studying the Tudors and Stuarts. In English literature they were reading *Wuthering Heights*, and studying poems like "Tiger Tiger, burning bright" from *Songs of Innocence* and *Songs of Experience* by the poet called William Blake. Flora even enjoyed the science lessons, sometimes. The only things she didn't like were Louise's two favorite subjects, sports and math.

Flora was so obviously happy that for a few weeks Aunt Jo worried about Louise more than she worried about her niece. Louise had not settled happily into her new school. It wasn't the schoolwork. She could manage that perfectly well. It was that, for the first time in her life, she was finding it difficult to make friends.

Partly this was because her best friend, Tracy Ann, had gone to a different school, and Louise, having lost her and Flora together, missed her badly. (That she found herself missing Flora, too, was not something she admitted, even to herself.) There was no one in her new class she really liked, or who seemed to like her. Perhaps she was too angry at this time to like anybody much. Perhaps it was because she was so angry that no one much liked her.

It did not help that Louise was the biggest girl in her class by far. Keith New started shouting out, "Hullo,

Dolly Parton," whenever he saw her, while his friend Peter Blackston suggested she get herself photographed topless for pinup pictures. Louise became so self-conscious that she started wearing big sweaters to hide her shape.

All this, of course, she blamed on Flora. Not that Flora seemed to notice. She kept on doing her Latin, reading her books. Louise grew angrier by the minute. But then, in the second week of school, she was rescued—it seemed like rescue—by Marilyn and her friends.

These three girls weren't first- or even second-year students. They were third year. "Hullo, little first year," they said, advancing upon Louise one morning in the playground. "Hullo, not-so-little first year," added the tallest of them, looking her up and down. When Louise opened her mouth to snap back, this same girl said in a much more friendly, almost wheedling voice, "Keep your hair on, first year. What's your name?"

"Louise," Louise said, reluctantly, staring her straight in the face.

"What a *sooper* name, Louise. How about we call you Lulu?" the girl asked. Though her voice was mocking, the expression on her face seemed friendly enough. She had long legs, half-shut, glinting blue eyes, and tangled fair hair. She was pretty, Louise had to admit. She also checked the sniggers of the other two girls with one wave of her hand. "The little fat one's Jacki," she informed Louise. "The stringy one's Lisa. And I'm Marilyn." Jacki and Lisa were smiling at Louise now, too. It was as if all the three of them wanted was to make Louise like them.

From then on Louise spent most of her time outside class with Marilyn, Jacki and Lisa. Doing things with them made her feel much better. Often they were the kinds of things her mother did not approve of. Her three new friends flattered Louise. They told her she was a good sport when she agreed to try smoking with them behind the bike shed. They made her persuade Jo to let her have her ears pierced. They offered her hair gel so she could make her short hair stand straight up on end. They encouraged her to turn her school skirt over at the waist till it was as short as theirs. (Louise always turned it down again, before she got home. Why does Mum have to be so old-fashioned? she thought.) They insisted she come shoplifting with them and dared her to take part. Louise did once come out of a shop with a roll of mints; but that was all. So far they hadn't made her sniff glue, but they talked about it often enough. Louise was fascinated by their daring. So much for brainy, wimpy Flora, she thought.

She was almost happy again, until one day, two weeks or so later, Marilyn, Jacki and Lisa saw her walking along the street with Flora in her still new-looking uniform. Next day they tackled her about it.

"Who's your fancy friend, Lulu?" they asked. "Any minute now with friends like that you'll be much too grand for us. Lulu, Lulu, Lulu," they chanted. It didn't sound so friendly anymore. They jostled her. One of them, Jacki, even gave her a sly pinch. But Louise wasn't going to let Flora drive away her new friends. She took her nose in her fingers, sniffed ostentatiously, and said, "Doesn't she stink. Doesn't she look like a nerd. That git's my sister, unluckily for me." And then she added, "Not even my real sister; she's my cousin, she's adopted." She was having an effect. The sly grins began to seem more for her than against her. And now she heard herself saying—she was instantly ashamed, but could not stop herself—"Her mum and dad weren't married; she's illegitimate—she's . . ." Here Louise hesitated, briefly; even about horrible Flora this was going too far. All the same, seeing the curiosity on her listeners' faces, she could not resist it. Hitching up her already short skirt, she confided, in a whisper, "My nerdy sister's a—*bastard*."

Marilyn's mother wasn't married, as it happened. Nor were the parents of several other children Louise knew. But she wouldn't have thought of calling any of *them* bastards, any more than she would have dared call Marilyn herself one. But this did not stop her in Flora's case.

"Wow," Marilyn said, stabbing at the ground with her foot. "Wow, Louise. That's ace. That's wicked. Your sister's a bastard. Hey, guys. Let's get her."

The glee she saw in Marilyn's face pleased Louise at first. So much for brainy Flora, she thought. Let Marilyn get her. But after a while, she began to feel worried. All the years she had spent looking after Flora, before they'd started falling out, weren't so easy to put aside. There'd been people who'd tried to bully Flora before. And it had always been Louise who'd stopped them. "My sister's not so bad," she used to tell them, "even if she is too brainy for her own good. Even if she does keep her head stuck in a book. Flora's all right really."

Seeing Marilyn's expression, she found herself repeating in her head again, Flora *is* all right really. And to her annoyance, she walked home feeling not just pleasure at the thought of Flora's comeuppance—for she did feel it—but also shame and apprehension.

(

Chapter
Five

Flora, meanwhile, knew nothing about Louise's gang. She'd barely even noticed Louise's change in hairstyle. Aunt Jo did suspect that Louise had found some unsuitable friends. But she said nothing for now. And when she asked Flora if she, too, would like her ears pierced, Flora looked horrified and shook her head. A week or so later, walking home from school, head down as usual, she suddenly saw three pairs of legs blocking her way; one very thin pair, one fatter, slightly bow-legged pair, one very long pair. She stopped dead; waited. When the legs did not move, she reluctantly raised her head to see three girls in school uniforms just like Louise's standing in front of her. The long-legged one, Marilyn, was smoking a cigarette. As Flora looked up, she took the cigarette out of her mouth, pursed her lips, and blew smoke straight into Flora's face. The second girl, Jacki, much shorter and plumper, reached out and snatched the beret from Flora's head. She and the third, more timid girl, Lisa, ran off up the street throwing the beret back and forth.

Good thing it's the wrong time of year for my boater hat, Flora was thinking, confusedly, as she started to pursue them, her school bag banging against her back. At this moment she was more angry than anything. She was angry with Louise for not even being there to protect her, as usual. She was angrier still when Marilyn held out one of her long legs to trip her up. Flora stumbled, but managed to right herself. At once Marilyn grabbed her by the arm and pinched her hard. Flora wrenched her arm away and, almost crying now, out of shock as much as pain, continued to run after Jacki and Lisa. Marilyn let her go. But Flora could hear her still jeering behind her.

"Slag bucket," Marilyn was calling; "Snob"; worst of all, "Bastard." Not that it occurred to Flora, of course, that Marilyn was using that term because she knew about Flora's parents. Jacki and Lisa were slowing up now, as if to let her catch them. Flora reached up her hand for the beret flying over her head. But again Lisa got there first. Yelling with excitement, she threw the beret into the nearest front garden, behind a bush. Then all three girls ran off.

When she had retrieved her beret, Flora stood staring at the bush for a moment. It was a perfectly ordinary holly bush, its berries already beginning to turn red. Flora did not know much about plants or gardens, or thought she didn't. She recognized holly, of course, because of Christmas. But that was all. So why now did this mysterious name come into her head? She found herself saying it out loud, several times over, tasting the word across her tongue. "Ilex Aquifolium"; and again, "Ilex. Ilex Aquifolium." Latin, she recognized, with a shock. But she hadn't known any Latin before this term. And the Latin she had been taught at school was things like *mensa*, meaning "table," or *Amo*—"I love." She had not been taught the Latin name for holly. And how did she know, anyway, that what she'd said *was* the Latin name for holly?

The very thought of it made her start retching with terror. In a moment she did actually throw up.

Thereafter, up till half-term, there was scarcely a day when Flora was not tormented by Marilyn, Jacki and Lisa. Not that she knew their names yet. By now, though, she knew the shape of their heads, their hands, their legs, as well as she knew her own. She thought she saw, heard them, everywhere, even when she didn't. When, all too often, they were lying in wait, they threw mud at her, they jeered at her, they pinched her, they tripped her up. If she turned and tried to go home another way they ran after her shouting names; most usually, over and over, "Bastard, bastard." The worst week of all, though, they didn't even call her names. They lined up along the pavement hissing at her like snakes. She had no choice but to pass them, expecting to be tripped up, pinched, any moment. But the three did, said, nothing. They just kept on with that terrifying hissing until she was out of earshot, out of sight.

Flora still had not told anyone about it. Sometimes, she cried herself to sleep. Louise, hearing her, was ashamed and frightened. But she did not know what to do about it any more than Flora did. She tried to protect

Flora sometimes. Once or twice she'd hidden behind a corner, ready to rescue Flora if things went too far. It would be risky, she knew. She'd seen the way Marilyn, Jacki and Lisa treated people who went against them. As it was they'd stopped being quite so nice to her these days. Sometimes at school they almost ignored her. It made her feel angrier with Flora than ever. Hearing Flora weep from her bed against the opposite wall, she'd think, "Serves her right." At other times the sound made her feel so miserable she wanted to make up with Flora. She even tried to keep her part of the room tidy. Not that Flora seemed to notice.

Flora's headaches had returned now. So had the voices. Anything could set them off. A smell; a sound from what seemed like long ago. The memories came from places not the least like Hammersmith, and people whom, as Flora, she could not remember meeting. None of them called her Flora. They called her by the second name her mother had given her: Penelope.

Once, in particular, it happened. It was a fine Sunday afternoon. Louise had gone to visit her friend, Tracy Ann, from primary school. Grudgingly, and to Flora's surprise, she'd suggested that Flora come to visit Tracy Ann too. But Flora had shaken her head, and retired instead to sit on her bed with a book. The book was *The Wind in the Willows,* an old favorite, partly because Flora's copy had once belonged to her mother. These days she mostly read it to comfort herself when she was unhappy.

But *The Wind in the Willows* didn't comfort her today. Her mother's name was written on the flyleaf, and her name was of all names the one Flora did not want reminding of just now. When Jo came to find her she'd hardly read one word. Looking anxiously at Flora's pale face, Jo said, "It's a lovely afternoon, Flora. You shouldn't be hiding in here. How about a nice walk, just you and me down by the river?"

Though they were well into October already, summer had lingered this year. In the riverside gardens of Chiswick Mall, chrysanthemums and dahlias were flowering. The sun set the huge gilt knobs and curlicues on Hammersmith Bridge gleaming. Along the towpath the boathouses were open, rowing crews strained their way upriver, while toward Barnes Bridge, sailing boats darted like butterflies from one bank to the other. Taking a surreptitious bite of the chocolate flake bar hidden in the white vanilla heart of the ice-cream cone her aunt had bought her, Flora felt so much better, she did not bother to keep an eye open for Marilyn and her friends. Looking around at all the people enjoying the sun, she even forgot to check her mind for unwanted memories.

She was taken quite unaware, therefore, when it happened.

Close to the river wall, above the houseboats moored along the jetty, a painter was standing before an easel, holding a paint-daubed palette. He was too absorbed in his picture of Hammersmith Bridge to notice Flora and Aunt Jo peering over his shoulder. But even when they'd left him behind, Flora still kept on smelling his paints. An oily, fatty smell, at the same time thin and sharp, it reminded her of another painter, a much older man in a velvet cap. He too had stood before an easel, brushes in one hand, palette in the other. But he had held his palette with a long handle, instead of a thumbhole at one end. Also he had been working indoors instead of outdoors, under a window too high to see out of. He was so vivid in Flora's memory, suddenly, she could almost hear his voice. She could hear him calling her his "little beloved, his . . ." But she did not want to hear him say her name—or rather her second name; the one that was written on the flyleaf of her mother's book. She put up her hand to drive the name away.

She touched her head. As she did so, she expected for a moment to find herself wearing some kind of hat. She knew it was much too big for her, whatever it was. She could feel its frill tickling her forehead. At the same time, with the other part of her, the part walking toward Hammersmith Bridge on an autumn afternoon, she knew there was no such cap. She knew that her head was as bare as the glittering water beneath the bridge was suddenly empty of boats.

The next moment the memories had slid away. There was a little boy of four or so alongside them, playing with a Day-Glo pink Frisbee. When the Frisbee landed at her feet, Flora threw it back to the little boy and found herself saying, wistfully, "He makes me feel so old now. He makes me feel *ancient.*"

"What things you say, Flora," said Aunt Jo, looking at her sharply. "Whatever next?" Flora sighed. As she glanced behind her at the painter, another memory slid into her mind. This memory, though, did not come from the mysterious past, the past of her other name. *This* memory belonged to her past as Flora, from the time before her mother died.

"What happened to the picture, Aunt Jo? The one

Mum had, wrapped up in brown paper, in a box with some of her books. She showed it to me once. She promised it would belong to me one day. What happened to it?" she asked.

"It's only up in the attic, Flora. I'll get it down for you, if you like," Aunt Jo said.

But by now Flora had changed her mind completely. "No," she cried. "No, I don't want to see it. No, I don't. I don't want to see it, ever."

☾
Chapter
Six

Toward half-term, for Lousie at least, life started to improve a little. During one phys-ed class, the teacher said he wanted to train up an athletics team. Looking at Louise's size, he said she might make a discus or javelin thrower—was she prepared to stay after school to practice? Yes, Louise said eagerly, she was. She went to the gym twice a week from then on. It did not make up for her lack of friends entirely, but just the same it helped.

For Flora, on the other hand, things got worse and worse. Though she still enjoyed her schoolwork, that was all that she enjoyed. For the first time in her life she began to feel in need of friends.

The trouble was there was no one she wanted to be friends with. She'd thought there'd be lots of girls at this school who liked reading, too, who would swap books with her. But if some were like that they didn't say. Apart from having richer parents, grander accents, they seemed not much different from Louise's friends at primary school. They, too, liked clothes and pop music. They, too, giggled about boys.

Jo advised her to give these new schoolmates a chance. But Flora didn't know how to; Louise had always made friends for her in the past. By now, anyway, they all seemed to dislike her as much as she disliked them.

The weather had changed at last to autumn. The wind rose, came in squally gusts; most days it rained also. The girls in Flora's class congregated around the big old-fashioned iron radiator. For a few days, until the system got used to itself, it gave off a tired burned-dust smell, before settling down again for winter.

The Latin class, in which everything for Flora came to a head, took place in a little slip of a room without a radiator, at the back of the school hall. Its neglected, occasional look suited the subject well. These days not everyone in Flora's school learned Latin. Only those who chose, or whose parents chose for them to learn, did so. Flora had insisted that she definitely wanted to learn Latin. By now, alongside English and French, it had come to be almost her favorite subject.

Since the beginning of term, her class had met the present and future tense of regular verbs. (*Amo*, "I love," *amaro*, "I will love.") This week they were to be introduced to the imperfect tense. (*Amabo*, "I was loving.") As soon as the subject was announced, Flora put up her hand. As usual she had a question. But just as her many questions had always irritated her sister Louise, now, just as much, they seemed to irritate her classmates. She could not mistake the little intake of breath from her next-door neighbors, the groan immediately behind her. These days, she did not care.

"Yes, Flora," said the teacher, Miss Wainwright, smiling at her. Flora liked Miss Wainwright. Not all her teachers enjoyed Flora's thirst for knowledge the way Miss Wainwright appeared to. Maybe they suspected that Flora was being impertinent. Sometimes she was.

Despite teaching such an unfashionable subject, Miss Wainwright herself wasn't old, let alone old-fashioned. Far from it. She was even glamorous. Flora had heard one of her more dress-conscious classmates call the large purple-and-white sweater Miss Wainwright was wearing today, over a short, rather tight black skirt, "mega lush." And now she was smiling, saying "Yes, Flora?" in tones of the utmost interest.

"Why *imperfect?*" asked Flora. "Why should 'I was loving' be any more imperfect than 'I love' or 'I will love'?" She could hear titters growing around her. Still she did not care.

"Well, Flora, it's interesting you should ask that." Miss Wainwright paused here to fix a stern eye on whoever it was just behind Flora who had groaned audibly. "I know none of you learn grammar in English these days. That leaves us linguists doing the donkey work. Have any of you heard of the perfect tense, even if you haven't heard of the imperfect?"

Flora put up her hand again; this time she didn't wait for Miss Wainwright. "*I* have," she said.

"Well, if you have heard of it, you know why imperfect is called imperfect. The perfect would be 'I loved,' wouldn't it? So what's the difference between that and the imperfect, 'I was loving'?" Miss Wainwright asked. Flora put up her hand again. At this moment, Emma Pelham, the girl at the next desk, laid a note on Flora's desk in such a way that Ginny Black, her neighbor on the other side, would be sure to see it too. The note said: "I HATE KNOW-IT-ALLS. I WAS HATING KNOW-IT-ALLS. I HATED KNOW-IT-ALLS."

"What's imperfect about that, Flora?" whispered Emma Pelham. "What's imperfect about that?" She fell into a paroxysm of giggles. So did Ginny Black.

Flora ignored them. She looked at Miss Wainwright, saying eagerly, "Is it because 'I loved' means something you don't do anymore? It's finished. 'I *loved*.'" She was thinking only of language; not of what such words might mean. It was her classmates who thought of what the words could mean. "Who did you love, Flora? Was it a boy? Or was it Miss Wainwright?" whispered Ginny Black. "I wasn't loving Flora," whispered Emma Pelham.

Miss Wainwright, meanwhile, was saying, "That's it, Flora," in tones of excitement. "That's it exactly. Do you hear, everyone? 'I loved' is finished. It's perfect; unlike all of you lot." Here she did stop to glare at the more unruly members of the class. "'I was loving' means loving hasn't come to an end; it's imperfect. That's exactly it."

She turned to write the words on the blackboard. Her back to the class now, she could not go on protecting Flora. Ginny and Emma seized their chance. Along with everyone else in the room, it seemed to Flora, they began to hiss, reminding her all too well of the way Marilyn and Jacki and Lisa had hissed: "I was loving; I wasn't loving Flora . . ." Soon the "wases" and "wasn'ts" had gained such sibilance, such hiss, it sounded as if the classroom was full of snakes.

Flora put her hands over her ears. Hardly knowing what she was doing, she left her seat and started to march toward the front of the class, to where Miss Wainwright was standing. Chalk in one hand, eraser in the other, Miss Wainwright turned in a whirl of chalk dust, just as Flora reached the teacher's desk.

Flora, too, turned to face the class. Only one girl seemed not to be laughing at her now. An Indian girl called Piloo. She'd only turned up in the class this past week. It was Piloo, therefore, whom Flora fixed her eyes on, as she began to recite. What she recited surprised her as much as anyone else. She did not know the words, or thought she didn't. She scarcely even knew what she was doing.

"*Arma virumque, cano,*" she proclaimed. "*Troiae que primus ab oris Italiam fato profugus Lavinque venit Litora . . .*"

She paused for a moment. She would have gone on then, but Miss Wainwright came from the blackboard and protectively took her arm. Not that anyone was laughing at Flora any longer. Ginny, Emma and the rest looked scared if anything. Only the Indian girl did not look scared; she was staring at Flora with great interest. What was with Flora then? someone else whispered. Had she gone barmy?—she *looked* barmy. No one except Miss Wainwright, of course, recognized what Flora had been reciting; it was the beginning of Virgil's *Aeneid*, she told the principal later. But how could a little girl like Flora, who had never studied Latin before this term, know about that famous Roman poet, let alone know any of his most famous poem by heart? She'd recited in such an old-fashioned accent, too, not at all the one Miss Wainwright herself had been taught. When she felt Miss Wainwright's hand on her arm, moreover, Flora had turned to her a face that looked as if it was seeing no one, at least not anyone in this room. And with a brilliant smile, and in a high voice that might have come from a child much younger, she had cried out to someone no one else could see, "You see, Doctor Darwin, Papa did teach me. I did learn it; though you said I couldn't. He's going to teach me some more very soon." Then, falling to the floor, she'd fainted dead away, before the whole class.

(

Chapter
Seven

"Tell me about meeting my mother, Aunt Jo," Flora begged. She was lying on the sofa in the front room of the house on Cardew Road the following day. Aunt Jo had been summoned to the school after Flora had fainted. She had taken off the rest of that day from her job in the dry cleaners in King Street. Still more unheard of, she had also taken off the whole of today, Friday, in order to be with Flora. Now she smiled; "I've told you already, Flora," she said. "So many times." But she was never averse to telling Flora about her mother.

Flora of course knew the story almost by heart. She knew how, aged eighteen or so, her mother had run away from home and come to work as a telephonist alongside Aunt Jo. How hopeless she'd been as a telephonist. Aunt

Jo had been assigned to train her, and even when the training was over, had gone on covering up for her mistakes. How Flora's mother always had her head in a book, and as soon as she discovered that Jo liked to read, too, had begun lending her books to Jo.

In due course Jo would always say, "Don't forget, Flora, your mum was my best friend." Then, more often than not she'd look sad. And sometimes she'd add—she did today—"But I'm not sure if I was *her* best friend, inviting her home, introducing her to my brother Ray, your dad, Flora. He did her no good, he didn't. He was a right bad one."

Aunt Jo sighed here, smiled at Flora, and said, in a fond voice, as she always did, "But still, most clouds have their silver lining and this one did."

"You mean *me*, I was the silver lining," said Flora, as *she* always did. And, she burst out laughing, seeing herself wrapped around Aunt Jo's shoulder within a black velvet cloak. But today, looking at her more fondly than ever, Aunt Jo added, "Not just a silver lining. Golden more like. Do you know, Flora, I'd begun to think you'd forgotten how to laugh." Then she got up from her chair and hugged Flora, enveloping her in the dry-cleaning, bad-egg smell that seemed to hang around her even when she wasn't wearing her work clothes. Flora liked that nasty smell, because it always reminded her of Jo.

Afterward Jo stayed looking down at Flora, still lying there, on the settee. Flora hadn't been born yesterday. She knew that her aunt wanted to talk about what had happened at school; about her fainting. But Flora did not want to talk to Aunt Jo about any such thing. Not now. Not ever. So she said, hurriedly, "You're always telling me about my mum, Jo." (She did call her aunt "Jo," some-times. Sometimes, especially in front of her schoolmates, she called her "mum.") "So why don't you ever tell me about my dad? *How* was he a bad one?"

It was true that when asked about her brother Ray, Jo did tend to change the subject. Not that Flora asked often; it seemed disloyal to Uncle Frank, whom she thought of in most ways as her father. Even today, Jo said nothing at first. She just sat down on the chair where she had been sitting before, alongside the big umbrella plant that flanked the bookcases Frank had built, after Flora's mother died, to hold all her books. She picked up her cof-fee, sipped it, and at last said, "I don't tell you, Flora, because I don't like to tell you. Your dad wasn't much good for your mum or anyone. Even if he did love her, for a while at least. Even if she did love him."

"If he'd really been bad, she wouldn't have loved him," Flora said.

"If only life was so simple," Jo said, sighing once more. "But I suppose you've a right to know something, Flora. He was your dad. And he wasn't *all* bad either. He had a good side, a best side. That was what he showed your mum, up till she got pregnant; and then he did what he always did when things seemed too much trouble; upped and went.

"Fact was, you sounded like an encumbrance, Flora, and he never had liked what he called encumbrances, my brother Ray. Everything to him was an encumbrance. A job was an encumbrance. Except for his time in the army, he never kept a job more than a week or two. Even a driv-ing license was one—the first trouble he got into was driving a stolen car without a license. While as for a baby,

Flora—he couldn't be doing with that. Even if he did love your mum. So off he went."

Jo hesitated suddenly. Flora, glancing at her, recognized the small pursing of her lips; it meant that Jo was seeing her way to bringing up the one subject she'd wanted to bring up from the start. On the other hand, Jo, looking at Flora, must have recognized the expression Flora at once put on of not wanting to hear whatever it was.

"I tell you this, Flora," Jo said, regardless. "Your dad so hated encumbrances, even your mum's name was one to him. 'What did you do to get a name like that, Pen?' he'd say. He called her Pen, mostly. Even when he called her by her proper name, he wouldn't ever *say* it properly. 'Don't call me that,' she'd say. 'That's not how you say it.' But it wouldn't stop him. 'Penny-lope' he'd laugh at her. 'My little doll. My Penny-lope.' 'But it's Penelope,' she'd tell him."

Not wanting to hear that name, Flora stared at Jo more angrily than ever. Yet nothing could divert her aunt from this tricky subject.

"Been in your family awhile, the name Penelope, your mum said," she went on. "Penelope wasn't just your mum's name—or just your second name, Flora, for that matter," she added, as if Flora needed reminding. "It was the name of the little girl in your mum's picture. Don't you remember?"

It was no use for Flora to stare back at her coldly, asking loudly, "What picture?" Of course the one time her mother had taken it out to show her, the picture had not interested her much. A boring black-and-white print, it had been brown-spotted with damp and set in a wooden frame. Yet suddenly she remembered all too clearly the child it showed. She wished that she could not. Whether she liked it or not, she and the little girl in the white dress staring out at her from the stained paper shared a name, at the very least. And who knows that they did not share a whole lot more?

Chapter
Eight

Flora still did not want to discuss such ideas with her Aunt Jo. So she lay back on the settee, shut her eyes, and pretended to sleep. To her relief, she heard Jo going out of the room. The next moment, thinking she might have gone to fetch the picture down from the attic where she had stored it, Flora sat up abruptly. Was Jo going to force her to look at it? No, I won't, she thought. I can't. I'll scream. She thought of running out of the room, out of the front door. But then she felt too weak still and lay back. And in the end, Jo reappeared carrying nothing but two mugs of tea. "I've put two spoons of sugar in for just this once, Flora," she said.

For a while they sat together in silence. Flora sipped the sweet and milky brew, and looked over the top of the mug at the familiar room; at the books, the cheeseplant, the crinoline lady on the mantelpiece, alongside the huge shell she and Louise had saved up to give Jo on her birthday last year. There was a picture on the wall above the fireplace that her mother had presented to Jo as a wedding gift, before Flora was born. The picture was by William Blake, who also wrote the poems Flora was studying at school from his books called *Songs of Innocence* and *Songs of Experience*.

"Tiger tiger burning bright, in the forests of the night," she murmured to herself, eyeing the crazy-looking man the picture showed measuring the world with a pair of compasses. The man was Sir Isaac Newton, a famous scientist from long ago. As long ago as Penelope? Flora wondered. Longer?

But at last, reluctantly, she allowed herself to look at Aunt Jo. "Now then, Flora," Jo said firmly, "isn't it about time you and I had a talk?"

"What about?" asked Flora.

"Don't give me that, Flora. You know what about."

"It's not *my* fault," Flora said. "*I* can't help it."

"Help what, love?" Aunt Jo urged her gently. "Help what? All the Latin and that? Where's it come from? You can't help *what*?"

Flora shook her head, tears welling up. But she was not going to cry now, in front of Aunt Jo. Not if she could help it.

But in a moment she almost wished she had cried. Because if she had, Aunt Jo mightn't have started saying what she did; all of it concerning things Flora didn't want to hear about, either then or ever. About some program she'd seen on television—how it reminded her of Flora—

how she'd wondered if what was happening to children the program showed could have been happening to Flora.

"Reincarnation, it's called, Flora," Jo said. "The children in the program kept remembering things from lives before they were born, because they'd once lived as those people in past times. It was just like you remembered your Latin, Flora. And all those other things you talked about when you were little. That you hadn't ever known. The little white dog, for one. Oh, and once a big stove with blue pictures on it. And that Doctor Darwin. You never knew any Doctor Darwin, you never saw anything like that, living with us, or before when you were just with your mum, for that matter. You couldn't have done. Not unless, like those other children, you'd been alive before, a long time ago, as someone else. And come to life again now, as Flora. Reincarnation, like I said."

All the time, feeling very angry, Flora kept on staring at the picture of Sir Isaac Newton measuring the world. How dare Aunt Jo say such things, she was thinking. In the books she read, it was children who believed in such crazy ideas, not parents. Well, let her; she, Flora, didn't believe anything so stupid. Never mind the name whispered in her head; never mind the memories. Whatever the girl in the picture meant to her, it wasn't anything like that.

"I know what reincarnation is," she said coldly. "But I'm not anyone's reincarnation. I just get headaches sometimes. That's all. You're nuts."

Aunt Jo was almost pleading with her now. "But, Flora," she said. "How'd you explain it then? Because it happened. It did, Flora. You'd say, 'When I was little, I had a dog called Tray.' Or 'When I was little, I used to ride on my papa's knee.' And you used to talk about big gardens, and a fish pond. And once, that was the beginning of it, your mum took you to the Tate Gallery, and you saw a man in a picture and called him 'Papa.' Flora, you never knew a real dad, let alone a papa—no one these days calls a dad a papa, so why did you?"

"I expect I saw it on television," said Flora more coolly than ever.

That was as far as they got for the moment. Saying she was tired now, Flora lay down with her face to the back of the sofa. When she looked around Aunt Jo had gone, taking the cups of tea with her. Flora regretted her cup of tea. For, after all, she could not sleep. She lay with her nose pressed to the rubbed red plush of the sofa back, snuffing a faint scent of what?—cough drops? tobacco?—and thinking thoughts she'd have preferred not to think about the little girl in the picture who was called Penelope. If I really was Penelope in another life, who am I now? Flora or Penelope? she wondered. If I remember things of hers, like Latin, would she remember things that happened to me, like those horrible girls hissing at me? Of course not. She's not the same as me. She's not me.

Flora rolled over then, sat up; said out loud to the walls, the cheeseplant, the crinoline lady, to the scientist forever bending over his compasses, "What's happening now is that I keep hearing the name Penelope, because my second name is Penelope. That's all it is. That's all."

(

Chapter
Nine

The following week it was the half-term holiday.
Aunt Jo worked half days at holiday times. Louise and
Flora used to stay at home together while she was
working, or else they would go and sit in the dry cleaners
with her all morning. But the first morning of this half-
term Louise said she'd rather go and see Tracy Ann, her
friend from primary school. And another morning she
said she was going to see a friend from her new school—
to make things for Halloween next week, she told them.
On those mornings Flora went to the dry cleaners without her.

Kathy and Betty worked at the dry cleaners as well as
Aunt Jo. Betty served behind the counter along with
Aunt Jo. Kathy was the machinist; she sat at the sewing

machine in the window, most days. Some days another woman, Vida, sat there instead.

Flora hardly knew Vida, and quite liked Betty. But Kathy was different. Next to Aunt Jo, Kathy was one of the people that Flora liked best.

Kathy came from the Caribbean island of Grenada. She had arrived in England when she was only eighteen, many years ago. She'd been a skinny little thing then, she said; now she was quite fat. All the same, shown pictures of her dressed up for the Notting Hill Carnival in sequined purple shorts, sequined purple bra and enormous feather headdress, Flora hadn't thought, "Kathy looks fat, she looks ridiculous"; she'd thought, "She looks wonderful," for so Kathy did. Flora was always begging Kathy to show her yet again how she danced in the procession at the carnival—sometimes Kathy obligingly did so, swaying and wiggling all over the shop. Often, too, Kathy brought Aunt Jo great bags of rotis—a bit like fat pancakes, with a spicy lentil stuffing; delicious. And once she had come to Cardew Road and cooked a whole Caribbean meal for them; chicken curry, plantains, sweet potatoes. But she had never invited them home to eat with her there. Because of her husband, she said. Kathy didn't think much of her husband; or of men in general.

"Give you fancy talk they will," she'd say. "Next things you knows you's looking after babies and they's getting drunk and chasing after girls and then where are you?" Whereupon she'd give one of her great laughs and Aunt Jo would nod her head and say, "*Men*," equally meaningfully. "*Men*"—as she often did, when talking to Kathy. It surprised Flora. Aunt Jo never seemed to find Uncle Frank troublesome. He was rarely home, for one thing. Flora, who didn't find Uncle Frank troublesome, either, also wished he was at home more often. Why did fathers have to be so busy, she wondered.

In the past when Flora went to the cleaners she'd take her books, or whatever, and sit in the window of the shop alongside Kathy, talking to her some of the time, or else reading or drawing. Or else she would sit up at the counter alongside Aunt Jo and Betty. If they were busy she'd help them fill out the tickets for customers. Sometimes, best of all, she'd be allowed to flip the switch on the circular rail holding garments waiting to be picked up. It would start lumbering around, setting the clothes in their cellophane bags swinging and sighing.

But Flora didn't want to sit in the front this time. She didn't even want to sit up at the counter. The front of the shop was glass, right to the floor. If Marilyn or Jacki or Lisa walked past they would see her sitting there. And then what? This Monday morning, therefore, when Kathy patted the place beside her with her usual smile, Flora shook her head and went right past the counter and into the back where Aunt Jo was standing, talking to Ahmed, who worked the machines and pressed the clothes. "I think I'll work here this morning, Aunt Jo," Flora said hurriedly, plonking herself down on one of the chairs set out for the workers. "If I sit in the front I'll look out of the window all the time and not get any homework done."

And it was true, she did have a lot of homework. But she did not get much of it done in the back of the shop, either. The machines were working all the time, the men talking as they ironed, the radio playing Radio One or Capital Radio. It was very hot. When Kathy came past to fetch her coffee cup, she did not smile at Flora.

Next morning, on the way to the shop, Flora said to her aunt, "It's smelly out in the back. *And* noisy."

"Why don't you come out to the front then, like you always do?" Jo asked. Flora said nothing. But when she arrived at the cleaners, she got the high stool from the office, and for the rest of the week, settled herself at the counter with her books. By Friday morning, though she still kept a careful eye on the window, she had almost stopped fearing to see Marilyn, Jacki or Lisa. Even when a small fat dark girl came in around eleven o'clock, she failed to recognize her. Jacki was weighed down with grocery bags. Flora could never have imagined any of the three doing something so ordinary as shopping with their mothers.

Luckily Jacki was too busy arguing with her mother to have noticed Flora. She was still arguing as Flora looked around for cover. She jumped off her stool, pushed aside a tweed jacket and a silk dress, and plunged into the middle of the circular rack of cleaned garments. The next minute she was in the dark, quite hidden, but trembling.

She could hear the voices in the shop still. She could hear the faint grind of pop music from the radio in the back. The movement of the rack when it started up, the grind of the machinery, the swaying of the clothes, was all just as she expected. What she did not expect—she never did—were the headache bands that she felt beginning to fasten themselves about her head. They brought with them the usual voices—the usual whispered or wept-over name. Penelope.

And worse than that. For when Aunt Jo crossly parted the clothes and pulled Flora out from her hiding place, Jacki and her mother were still standing at the counter. Jacki recognized Flora now. Behind her mother's back she grinned nastily at Flora. Playing at being old friends, she pulled her over to the corner of the shop and hissed in her ear, "It's no good your hiding, bastard. *We* know where to find you. And we've got plans for you. Ace plans. Haven't we just."

(

Chapter
Ten

Louise, of course, knew something of what these plans were, and wished she didn't. She had hoped at the half-term holiday to get away from Marilyn and her friends. The problem was she was still so unpopular in her own class, she had no other school friends to go to.

One more reason for her unpopularity now was Marilyn, Jacki and Lisa. No one was anxious to sit next to Louise in class, or be her partner when they were asked to take partners. They did not want to bring on themselves the unwelcome attention of Louise's friends, the third-year bullies.

At half-term, too, Louise had hoped to be able to get together again with Tracy Ann, her best friend from primary school. But when she went around to Tracy Ann's house on Monday morning, she found her out with friends from her new school. It was the same on Tuesday. On Wednesday morning she met Marilyn in the street and Marilyn said, "You're coming around to my place tomorrow, aren't you, Lulu?" By then Louise was almost glad to accept the invitation; even though it was more of a threat than an invitation.

Marilyn lived in the untidiest place Louise had ever seen; but not just untidy. Louise was used to the house she lived in seeming loved in some way, just like the people. The apartment Marilyn lived in, however, didn't look loved in the least. The kitchen sink was full of dirty dishes. Every shelf, every surface was heaped with boxes, teaspoons, cans of food, paper tissues, milk bottles, newspapers, socks, panties, magazines. Nothing had a place of its own, or was in a place where you might expect to find it. Poor Marilyn, Louise thought. She was surprised to find herself feeling sorry for Marilyn.

Not that it appeared to worry Marilyn. "Now," she said, proceeding to clear two dirty mugs, a string vest and a copy of *Sporting Life* off the kitchen table. "What we're going to do today is plan for Halloween."

Louise knew about Halloween, of course. She'd made witches' hats at primary school, lit candles inside lanterns hollowed out of pumpkins. She'd put a sheet on her head and gone up and down the street with Flora, banging on people's doors, demanding trick or treat, hoping for a few smarties or mini crunchie bars, or even a 5- or 10-penny piece if she was lucky.

But this was not all that Halloween meant for Marilyn. Very soon it became clear that to Marilyn Halloween meant big business. No smarties or 5-penny pieces for her; she was after boxes of chocolates, £1 pieces—even £5 notes. And if she didn't get such things? Maybe that was the point, really. For what interested Marilyn still more than treats was tricks. Their job today was to devise costumes to frighten the life out of people, on the one hand; to devise tricks by which to punish their lack of generosity, on the other. Superglue on their door-mats, for instance; raw eggs or stink bombs through the slots for letters in their front doors; rude words written in phosphorous paint on the front of doors.

The more she heard of all this the more uncomfortable Louise felt. She knew what her mother would say about such goings-on. Jo had never much approved of Halloween, anyway. Still worse, Marilyn proclaimed what fun it would be frightening all those people they had it in for, including Louise's bastard sister, Flora.

Louise said nothing. She only knew she would have to protect Flora somehow. How, though, was another matter. Louise had never in her life before been frightened of any-one, but she was, she realized, frightened of Marilyn.

All the same, Marilyn was clever. Louise enjoyed mak-ing masks with her that morning in spite of everything. Even the glue pot Marilyn produced to help stick horns and ears and noses on the masks did not make her feel apprehensive. If Marilyn just spent her life making things, she thought, Marilyn would be all right, really.

But of course Marilyn never stuck to just making things. Toward the end of the morning, she picked up the glue pot and looked at it appraisingly; she looked at Louise, too, appraisingly. "How about a sniff, Lulu?" she said, teas-ingly. Fortunately, it was almost dinnertime by now; not only Louise was due home, Jacki and Lisa were also.

"See you tomorrow, Lulu?" asked Marilyn, as Louise went out, holding up for her the death's head mask on which she was just then working. "See you," replied Louise. Suddenly, though, going around to Marilyn's seem the very last thing she wanted. And when she climbed the stairs of the apartment building next morning and got no answer from Marilyn's doorbell, she felt more relieved than let down, let alone disappointed.

This was the very day, of course, that Jacki went shopping with her mother, the day Flora hid among the cleaning.

Afterward, sighing, Aunt Jo took Flora and her headache home and put her to bed. Once Flora murmured the name Penelope—"I'm not Penelope," she muttered—making Jo more certain than ever that in some way she really was. She was sure that for Flora's own good, she must be persuaded to acknowledge that she was the reincarnation of the little girl in the portrait.

She resolved to try some drastic measures. Louise came home to find the ceiling trapdoor that led into the attic open, and two unfamiliar objects lying on the floor of the landing. As she reached the top of the stairs, her mother came down the folding ladder backward, carrying an equally unfamiliar suitcase, very shabby and old-fashioned and decorated with the remains of labels.

One of the other two objects was a package, a big square flat thing wrapped in brown paper. When Louise put out her hand to pull the paper off, her mother slapped her hand away. She picked up the package and tucked it under her arm. She picked up the suitcase in her other hand and motioned at Louise to take the one thing left. Upside down on the floor this had looked like a square wooden box with a handle. But now Louise saw it was a miniature chest of drawers standing on little wooden legs. Its drawers had little brass handles and were decorated with inlaid wooden flowers and geometric designs, scattered haphazardly. It rattled as Louise shook it, as if there were things inside the drawers. Louise could not resist moving her hand to one little brass handle. But her mother frowned and said, "Leave that, Louise. These things aren't yours to look at; they were Flora's mother's, so now they're Flora's." And then she added, thoughtfully, "I hid all these things away after Flora's mum died, you know. It did seem best. But now I won-der if it *was* best."

They took everything down to the kitchen. When Aunt Jo went back upstairs to check on Flora, Louise, too impatient to wait, started to pull the paper off the big flat package that looked as if it might hold a picture. She really only meant to take a peek, then put the wrappings back. But in her hurry she pulled the paper so hard it tore right across. By the time her mother returned to say Flora was still asleep, there was no means of concealing the face that stared almost defiantly out from the polished wooden frame; a face topped by a floppy cap much too big for the size of the small head.

"Doesn't she look like Flora?" Jo said. Louise shook her head violently, and began trying to read the faded spi-dery writing at the bottom of the picture.

"J. Reynolds pinxit," she read on one side (what was that funny word, *pinxit?*—Latin?), on the other "Savage del": whatever that meant. But in rather bigger, clearer writing in the middle was written the name of the little girl also. "Penelope," she read. "Penelope Boothby."

"There," her mother was saying, behind her, in a tone almost of triumph. "Penelope. You see, that's her. That's who Flora remembers being. That's how it is."

(

Chapter
Eleven

"Like how?" Louise asked, her tone daring her
mother to say more. Even if she didn't believe a word of
it, she still did not like to imagine she was sharing a bedroom with someone who might be someone else. If Flora
wasn't just Flora, if she was also this little two-hundred-
year-old girl staring out at Louise now with grave eyes,
her mouth as fine cut as that of an old-fashioned china
doll, then who *was* Flora? What ghost, what phantom had
tossed and turned in the bed next to her own, every night
in the week, all Louise's life? What nonsense, she told
herself. No matter how different Flora was from her, she
was still just Flora. She was no more this Penelope than
Marilyn when wearing her mask had really been a red-
lipped female devil.

Aunt Jo had propped the picture up now on the kitchen work surface, next to the electric kettle, and also the wooden cabinet with its brass handles. She and Louise were both staring at it so intently, that neither heard the still sleepy Flora come into the kitchen. They jumped around, startled, when she cried out, "What are you doing? That's my mother's picture. I told you I didn't want to look at it. I told you." The next minute she had rushed around the table and turned the picture's face to the tiled wall.

Aunt Jo picked up the little wooden chest then and handed it to her. "Come on, Flora. Surely you want to know what's inside this," she urged her.

"As long as you put the picture away," replied Flora, calmly but insistently. "I told you I didn't want to see that picture. I told you."

She wouldn't have been allowed to speak to her mother in such a way, thought Louise, crossly; so why should Flora be allowed to? But Flora was. And the next moment the picture was outside the door, while Flora, pulling each little brass handle one by one, was emptying the contents of the drawers onto the kitchen table. Inside they smelled musty, spicy, as of long-ago spices, long-ago dust. And each held buttons of some kind; brass buttons in one drawer, china ones decorated with flowers in another, black buttons studded with little glass jewels like diamonds in a third, bone buttons in the fourth and last.

It was hard to say which of them, Flora or Louise, was the more pleased by all these treasures. For they felt like treasures. Aunt Jo, meanwhile, picked up the seemingly empty cabinet and, shaking it a little, said, "This would polish up nicely. Wait a moment," she added, pulling out the bottom drawer. "What's this? I don't think you got everything out." And there, sure enough, wedged into the back of the drawer, was something wrapped in yellow tissue. Inside was a walnut shell. The shell opened when Jo drew it from the paper. To the surprise of all of them, it had been hinged like a box, and lined with faded green velvet. On the velvet nestled two little white things. "Teeth; baby teeth," Jo said.

"This was my mother's box. Maybe they were my mother's baby teeth," said Flora. Louise thought that was a scary idea, herself, though Flora didn't seem to. Under her breath she muttered to herself—she was joking, of course—"Maybe they're Penelope's baby teeth."

If Flora heard her, she made no sign. Jo, however, shook her head warningly at Louise. She put on the kettle, and brought cookies out of the Silver Jubilee box. Marzipan-topped ones for Louise, her favorite; jaffa cakes for Flora. Flora had hated the taste of almonds in the marzipan ever since she could remember.

"Perhaps some of these buttons were on my mother's clothes when she was little," said Flora.

"Maybe," said Aunt Jo. "But she used to play with them when she was a little girl, Flora, she told me so, so maybe they were older than that."

"Maybe they were on Penelope's clothes," Louise said.

This was too much for Flora. Glaring at Louise, she jumped up from the table, rushed out of the room and almost fell over the leather suitcase sitting in the hall outside. She hesitated for a moment. But then with a wary glance at the open kitchen door behind her, she clicked its brass catches open, and threw the lid right back. The smell of the button cabinet was nothing to the smell of mold and must and dust that rose from the clothes that filled it.

They were quite ordinary clothes some of them—aertex shirts, for instance, nylon stockings, faded T-shirts. There was a pair of satin shorts, too, and a pair of embroidered boots. But underneath all these were much older things. Flora forgot her rage, and wrapped one of three tasseled shawls around herself. Prancing back into the kitchen to show it off, she found she had wrapped around her not only the swathe of dark red silk, but also the ancient, sad smell of the whole box.

"I remember your mum wearing that shawl, Flora," Aunt Jo said. "I remember her wearing almost all those clothes."

"But they're all old clothes," objected Louise. "Dressing-up clothes. You can't wear things like this. Not to go out in."

"Well, Pen wore them," Aunt Jo said. "A little left-over hippy she was. She liked beads and lace and tassels, all sorts. These were her family dressing-up clothes, so she said, that she brought with her when she came to London. 'Course, some of this stuff she bought herself. The T-shirts and so on. And the hot pants of course. I remember her buying this," Aunt Jo added, holding up a faded purple T-shirt with a scoop neck; "I remember her buying this, too—" Now she was holding up an embroidered cap. "And I remember her wearing it. She looked lovely in that cap. It'd suit you, too, Flora. You're beginning to look a bit like your mum now, why don't you try it on?"

But Flora did not want to try it on. She did not know whether she liked the idea of looking like her mother. She continued to turn the clothes over till she'd all but reached the bottom of the suitcase. A yellow silk dress seemed much older than anything else that she'd discovered. Its silk ripped as Flora lifted it. Underneath lay something made of discolored lace. Flora took it out and held it up. Immediately, she wished that she had not. "A mob cap," she heard Jo murmur. Its lace torn and yellow with age, the cap was still just like the one worn by Penelope in the picture that Flora went on refusing to look at.

Flora thrust it back into the suitcase and told Aunt Jo, almost rudely again, to take the suitcase and the picture straight back to the attic. Aunt Jo looked at Flora and sighed, but didn't say anything. Rather than replacing them in the attic, however, she hid the picture behind the wardrobe in her room and pushed the suitcase under her bed. She had a feeling—Louise heard her telling her father this—that Flora might want to look at them both sometime.

"What a load of nonsense, Jo," Louise's father said as usual; just what Louise wanted to think herself. The aged smell of the cabinet, of the suitcase, of their contents, still in her nostrils, she decided she didn't really like old things. The thought of a time long past in which you weren't, but with which, in Flora's case, you might be connected, was quite uncomfortable, she decided. All the nicest, most pleasurable things were shiny and new, weren't they? At least she had always thought so.

☾

Chapter Twelve

It was still four days to the thirty-first of October when school started again. Halloween was not made much of in Flora's school. It never occurred to her that Jacki's threats referred to it. Apart from Jacki, she had not encountered anyone in Marilyn's gang for the whole of the holiday week, nor did she encounter them for several days thereafter. Despite the threats she even began to hope that they were growing tired of hounding her. She found it all the easier to be hopeful because, for the first time in her life, she'd started to make a friend, on her own, without Louise's help.

This friend, Piloo, was the Indian girl Flora had fixed her eyes on while reciting Latin; the one who had looked at her, nodding, as if she knew what it was all about. After the holiday Flora found herself eyeing Piloo with interest. Just as Piloo, she saw, eyed her.

It hadn't seemed to worry Piloo one jot that, till now, she too had had no friends. She showed not the slightest desire to fit in. At recess, she walked around the playground like an empress with a train of invisible servants behind her. In class she sat smiling coolly, turning out work that almost always, along with Flora's, got the top marks for whatever it was, even science and math. She hadn't shown any interest in Flora, either, to start with. But the first day after school began again, Flora found Piloo not only sitting beside her, but also starting to say something friendly.

Piloo was different from anyone else in the class. It was not just that she was cleverer, certainly not that she was Indian—the two other Indian girls in their class seemed just like all the others, apart from their dark hair and eyes. Very quickly it became clear to Flora that Piloo was different in some of the ways that she herself was different.

For instance, though like Louise she wore small gold rings in her pierced ears, Piloo didn't seem any more interested in clothes or pop music than Flora. On the other hand she had plenty to say about the books and poems they were reading in English; *Wuthering Heights*, "Tiger Tiger," for instance. It was after the talk Piloo gave in their English class about *Wuthering Heights* that she and Flora struck up their first real conversation.

Piloo spoke the most precise, elegant English Flora had heard from anyone, except perhaps the queen; though the queen's voice didn't have the somewhat singsong intonation that Flora heard in Piloo's. Piloo said this was because she had so very recently come from Calcutta.

Piloo's grandmother had been ill; the family had stayed in India with her till she was better, that was why Piloo had been late starting school, she said.

"But my grandmother is quite well now, Flora, thank you very much for asking," Piloo added, not that Flora had asked. Piloo was not mocking her, however. It was just Piloo's way of speaking. Flora, enchanted, could have listened to her for hours.

Compared to herself, too, Piloo seemed to know so much, had traveled to so many places. Flora, who had hardly been anywhere except London, loved hearing Piloo talk about India, about Bangkok, Hong Kong, Washington, all places she'd visited with her parents. At the same time Piloo knew nothing about other things. She had hardly seen any television, for instance—"Tee Vee," she called it. When the girls in her class talked about "Neighbours" or "Top of the Pops" or "The Bill" she looked mystified. It wasn't just that Piloo had been in England so little. She didn't watch television at home in either Calcutta or London. Her mother wouldn't let her, she said, except for the news sometimes and nature programs. "And of course my mother is quite right," said Piloo. "How much more there is to find in books. Television is so superficial."

She was the first friend Flora had ever had who used words like *superficial*. If it occurred to her that in saying such things, Piloo sounded a little priggish, she did not let it bother her. She replied, "I like books better too." Because on the whole she did like books better. On the other hand she also liked settling down with her family to watch "Neighbours," say. It felt so cozy, so safe, leaning against Aunt Jo's knee. Even the murders, rapes and bombings that so often followed on the six o'clock news could not spoil that altogether. Only when such horrors set her hearing in her head those mysterious, awful words, "Eat or be eaten," did she stop feeling safe and begin to shudder.

Before long, too, Piloo was making Flora tell her what happened in last night's episode of "Neighbours." In return she told Flora stories about Calcutta. She talked about the Festival of Lights—Diwali. She told Flora how clean Hammersmith was compared to Calcutta. She talked about "the servants." For in India, of course, Piloo's family had a great many servants. Flora had never met anyone before who was used to servants. She pushed away faint memories that stirred in her when Piloo was talking about them; memories of a man in knee breeches and white stockings, of girls in print dresses and white caps. They had nothing to do with her, Flora, had they? She'd seen such people in some film on television. They didn't belong to any past of her own.

On the Thursday of their first week of friendship Piloo asked Flora to come to tea next day, October thirty-first. It was the first time anyone from that school had invited Flora home. Aunt Jo seemed almost as pleased about it as Flora herself. As for Flora, only the groups of children dressed up in white sheets or witches' hats that she and Piloo saw when they were walking back from school together reminded her that the date was Halloween. Nor, until they turned in at the gate, did she realize that Piloo was taking her home through the cemetery; the one in which Flora's mother was buried.

Flora stopped still then, right in the middle of the gate.

"What's the matter, Flora?" said Piloo. "Are you afraid to walk among dead people? I never thought *you* would be superstitious."

"I'm *not* superstitious," said Flora. But she did not think Piloo knew her well enough yet to be let into all the secrets of her life. So she started walking again, trying to look unconcerned. Fortunately, the path they needed to take kept to the old part of the cemetery, the part with the elaborate monuments; angels and urns, and models of open books. Flora's mother was buried in the modern part of the cemetery, on the far side.

The path turned a corner. Here, closed in by sooty brick walls, the cemetery seemed more dismal than ever. Leafless trees stood about a group of headstones set in the center of the area. They were very small headstones, and leaned against one another as if to comfort each other's grief. The inscriptions commemorated little children called things like Reggie and Cyril, Violet and Nancy, all of them dead for fifty years at least. The inscription on Reggie's tombstone read: THE SUNSHINE OF OUR LIVES GONE TO LIGHT UP THE ANGELS. Counting up the time between the dates of his birth and death, Flora found that he'd lived five years and three months, precisely.

Five years was a long time looked at in one way, she thought. Five years in her life seemed forever. But when five years—or less—was the whole of a life, it seemed like nothing; like no time.

According to Flora's mother, Penelope, the little girl in the portrait, had lived for not much more than five years. Staring at the small gravestones, Flora remembered the other stories her mother had told her about Penelope.

But though she had liked hearing these stories when she was little, she didn't want to think of them now. Five years, she thought again, hearing in her head as she did so the sound of the woman crying for her Penelope. Five years, eleven months, only.

（

Chapter
Thirteen

Piloo lived in an apartment in a big red block of apart-
ments, overlooking trees and tennis courts. It was not a
little apartment; far from it. The high-ceilinged rooms
were as tall as Flora's whole house. The gold carpet covering the living-room floor was big enough to cover all the
floors in No. 37, Cardew Road.

Even though Piloo's room was twice the size of the
one Flora shared with Louise, she didn't have to share it
with anyone. Apart from Piloo's bed and dressing table, it
contained a big desk, on which stood a small new computer. Piloo said her father was going to show her how to
work it any day. On a narrow shelf above the desk a small
but elaborately carved figure with the head of an elephant
danced on a man's bent legs. "That's Ganesha, Flora," said

Piloo, seeing Flora's eyes on it. "That is one of our Hindu gods." But she didn't explain further.

There was nothing else the least bit Indian in the room. The bed and chair covers were patterned with green leaves and pink roses. Almost the whole of the wall opposite the bed was taken up by a bookcase, full of Piloo's books. When Flora went to look at them Piloo said, "Later, Flora, it's teatime now, aren't you hungry? I always feel so hungry in this cold climate."

Tea was set out in a room next door to the big living room. "We aren't standing on much ceremony in our home, but we wouldn't think of giving a guest, such as your good self, Flora, a meal in the kitchen," Piloo's mother, Mrs. Bannerjee, said.

She looked very like Piloo, apart from being much taller. Rather than Indian clothes, she wore jeans and a tight polo-necked red tunic. Her Aunt Jo could never have worn anything so tight-fitting, Flora thought. Mrs. Bannerjee's long, dark, very glossy hair was held back with jeweled combs. Despite the big rings she wore on her fingers, she didn't look much older than Piloo.

Though Flora had wondered if she'd have an Indian tea at Piloo's house, what she got was sandwiches, fruitcake and chocolate cookies set out on fine china plates.

"We are having an English tea, in your honor, Flora," Mrs. Bannerjee said. "Please help yourself to a cucumber sandwich. Don't be polite. Be taking two at least. There are no egg sandwiches, I am afraid. We are Hindus, you see, Flora. We don't eat eggs. We don't eat meat."

Piloo said, "Though we are vegetarians, we may eat meat in England. My grandmother said that in England it's polite to eat what we are given. She said that in any case we can only be proper Hindus in India."

"But we still prefer not to eat meat, or eggs," said Piloo's mother. "I ask myself, if I am eating such things, if I stop trying to be a good Hindu even in England, what will I come back as in my next life?"

"Maybe you'll come back as an English person, Mummyji," said Piloo gravely. Flora had the impression that Piloo was, very politely, teasing her mother.

Again her mother turned to Flora. "You see, Flora, reincarnation is something else we Hindus believe in," she said. "But what kind of life you return to, who you are reincarnated as, depends on how well you have led your old life. Whether you have been charitable, polite to your parents, whether you have eaten the right things, done many pujas, and so on."

Horrified at hearing that hateful word *reincarnation* here, right out of the blue, Flora picked up a cucumber sandwich, and, attempting to swallow it at a gulp rather than nibble at it politely the way she'd been trying to do before, started choking. Throwing out a hand then, she knocked over her cup of tea. The delicate china broke. The hot tea poured into her lap, all over her school skirt and sweater. She leaped to her feet and stood there, soaking wet, almost crying with embarrassment. Couldn't she get away from Penelope anywhere? she thought. Was there nowhere in the world she'd feel safe?

Piloo's mother was kind, though. She said not to worry one little bit about the cup; accidents do so easily happen. And Flora must change out of her wet clothes at once. She would be getting influenza, Mrs. Bannerjee worried, she would be getting pneumonia. It would not do at all, she said.

Before Flora knew what was happening she found herself, stripped to her underpants in Piloo's room, wrapped in Piloo's woolen dressing gown. Piloo's mother had pulled open a drawer, was picking out Piloo's sweaters to find one that might suit Flora.

Flora was amazed at the amount of clothes Piloo had. There were not only skirts, jeans, dresses, but also some much brighter, richer-looking silk clothes, some even embroidered with what looked like gold thread. Clothes for princesses, Flora thought, Indian princesses. At that very moment, looking at her closely, Piloo's mother said, "Do you know, Flora, I think you would look so pretty in Punjabi dress."

Punjabi dress—"shalwar khameez," Mrs. Bannerjee called it—consisted of a long tunic top and a pair of matching slightly baggy trousers, tied with a drawstring at the top. Mrs. Bannerjee picked out for Flora a particularly splendid set made of a rich scarlet silk. It had gold embroidery at its neck, and an elaborate printed pattern running along the sleeves, along the hem of the tunic and the trousers also. "Try the shalwar, Flora," she urged her, handing over the trousers.

Putting the garment on, first the shalwar, then the tunic—the khameez—felt like dressing up to Flora. She was reminded of the time she'd swathed herself in the red silk shawl from her mother's dressing-up suitcase. But that had smelled musty and unused. These clothes smelled fresh, they rested delicately on her skin in this warm place. Flora had never in her life been interested in the clothes she wore. But now, in Piloo's room, dressed in these princess clothes, she found herself longing to see what she looked like. When Piloo's mother cried, "Come now, Flora, you are looking gorgeous, you must come and admire yourself at once," she allowed herself to be led, without protest, along the passage to Mrs. Bannerjee's own room, and stood in front of a long mirror.

The faint incense smell that filled the apartment was not faint in here at all. The source of it appeared to be a kind of altar set up in a corner. At its center stood the god with an elephant's head, Ganesha, wearing a yellow-and white garland. Was it the smell that confused Flora's senses, she wondered, staring at herself. Just what, just *who*, had she expected to see staring back at her in the soft, pinkish light of this room? Had she expected to see, looking out of the mirror at her, an altogether different, Indian Flora? An Indian princess Flora?

But alas, it was not so. The girl staring back at her out of the mirror was still Flora. Yet, strangely, she felt quite happy about being *this* Flora. The richness of the scarlet silk might not have made her look Indian in the least. But Piloo's mother had been quite right to choose such a color. It suited her dark hair, her white skin. For the first time in her life Flora felt not only interested in, but almost pleased by the way she looked.

Afterward, while they were waiting for Flora's clothes to dry, Piloo and Flora went to Piloo's room to do their homework.

They began talking to each other afterward, the way friends talk. Flora had never in her life before talked that way to anyone. She didn't tell Piloo about Penelope. But she did tell her that her Aunt Jo believed like Mrs. Bannerjee in reincarnation.

"And all because of a program on the television," she said. "A crazy Tee Vee program; would you believe it, Piloo." But now her mother wasn't there to tease, Piloo didn't seem to think such beliefs *were* crazy. She said that sometimes in India children were born with birthmarks just like the knife or bullet wounds suffered by the dead people they used to be in their past life.

What did Penelope die of then? Flora asked herself, mockingly. A bang on the head, was it? She knew there was no scar anywhere on her head. On the other hand, it did occur to her to wonder, for the first time, if the headaches she suffered were connected in some way to the manner of Penelope's death.

She saw Piloo looking at her curiously. "There's been something I've always wanted to mention to you, Flora," she said, smiling. "That day in the Latin class when you recited Virgil, I thought *you* sounded like the children in India. The reincarnated ones."

"Oh yes, Piloo," said Flora, coldly. "Oh yes, I'm a reincarnation all right. I'm the reincarnation of Isaac Newton."

Piloo did not pursue the matter. Instead she took Flora back into her mother's living room and, opening the very new-looking piano, began teaching her to play a chopsticks duet. But when Flora put tentative fingers to white notes and to black she found them falling into different places, one after another. Not only were they playing a tune; still more amazingly, both her hands were working together to play it. It was a simple tune, but a tune, definitely, and very familiar, though not familiar to her as Flora.

"I thought you'd never learned the piano," Piloo said.

"No, I haven't," said Flora, almost in tears. "I haven't." Taking her treacherous hands off the keys, she stared at them in such horror, she hardly heard Piloo saying smugly, "Someone else must have learned, then."

Louise was out trick-or-treating with Marilyn and her gang meanwhile. They'd started by looking for Flora. Louise had not told them that her cousin wasn't going straight home. She'd let them hang around in the usual place until they grew bored by waiting. "Not to worry, Lulu," they said, they'd get her bastard sister some other time.

Apart from the masks, it wasn't so different trick-or-treating with Marilyn's gang from doing it with anyone else. The main difference was that Marilyn took most of the spoils rather than sharing them with the others. Also they had a supply of eggs with them in an egg-box, and threw these at the front doors of people who weren't in. Or who, in Marilyn's view, pretended they weren't in. Or who were in, but didn't, in Marilyn's view, give generous enough treats.

The eggs were nothing, Marilyn said, compared to the much worse tricks she had up her sleeve, but she was keeping *them* until after dark. She was wearing her devil mask at the time. Louise escaped as soon as she could, muttering something about her mother.

Flora, shortly after, on her way home in Mrs. Bannerjee's Volvo, saw groups of children wearing sheets, masks, witches' hats in almost every side street. Piloo's mother was saying how interesting she found such English folklore. Flora, however, clutching a little figure of Ganesha she'd found on the dashboard, hardly heard a word. The groups of children dressed as ghosts made her think of real dead souls wandering the streets tonight. For that was the meaning of Halloween, wasn't it?—it wasn't just to do with witches and dressed-up children. Did all dead souls, she wondered, expect to be reborn?

Those children buried in the cemetery, for instance: had they been reborn in other people, the way Aunt Jo thought Penelope had been reborn in her? she wondered. And if they hadn't been, *why* hadn't they been? Maybe they all had been. Maybe most people were lucky enough not to know they had used to be someone else in a past life, she thought, fingering for comfort the little figure of the Hindu god.

There was yet another group of trick-or-treaters standing at the bottom of Cardew Road, three of them this time, wearing masks: one devil mask; two skulls. Flora, though, safe in Mrs. Bannerjee's Volvo, scarcely gave them a single glance.

Cardew Road was a narrow street. It had grown much more fashionable than when Jo and Frank bought their house from the council, and much more expensive. These days shiny new cars were parked along its whole length. If two cars driving along it met halfway, one always had to back to let the other through.

Tonight, when Mrs. Bannerjee turned into Cardew Road, there was another car directly behind her. The other driver was impatient, moreover. He honked at Mrs. Bannerjee when Flora pointed out her house and she started to slow down.

"I will have to park around the corner, Flora, and walk

back. What should I say to your mother if I did not see you safely right to your own front door?" Mrs. Bannerjee said.

"It's okay," said Flora. "I've got my key out, look. Just leave me by the gate. It'll be all right."

"It will not be all right, Flora," said Mrs. Bannerjee. "It will not be all right at all."

At that moment the driver behind honked again. At the same time—though none of them noticed—the three masked figures drew closer. They were now only two houses away, grouped by the gate.

Piloo, too, was impatient. "Oh, Mummyji, you are so old-fashioned," she said, if politely. "Flora walks home from school by herself every day. She'll be all right."

The car had stopped now. Flora had the door open, was scrambling out, her school bag in one hand, her key in the other.

"Thanks for tea, Mrs. Bannerjee," she said. "It really is all right."

The car behind honked for the third time. Flora, now standing inside her own front gate, flourished her key once more to show her friends. Mrs. Bannerjee, still looking worried, glanced back over her shoulder at the car behind—another Volvo, Flora noticed. Then she waved, and drove off. As her taillight disappeared around the corner Flora tried to shut the gate with the hand that held her door key. At the moment the gate clicked shut, she dropped the key on the path.

At first when she bent to pick it up, she could not see it. She scrabbled blindly in the dirt, panic-stricken suddenly for no good reason. She was just six feet from her own front door, after all, in her own street. But then, as her hand fell on the key at last, she heard just above her head the rusty hinges of the gate start squealing.

"Scream all you like, bastard. This is *your* Friday the thirteenth. This is your own video nasty. We've got you now," hissed the all-too-familiar voice. For Flora, scrambling to her feet to find herself gazing straight into the devil mask, had shrieked out loud. "Wanted a treat did you? That was a terrific car you were riding in. Well, from now on, treats are history; all you're going to get is tricks. TRICKS," Marilyn shouted, thrusting the devil horns, the thick devil lips right into Flora's face.

Flora had backed right up against her front door now. As the sheeted figures reached out their hands to her, she managed to twist herself around sufficiently to find the bell. Before they could stop her she'd pressed it over and over. The figures hesitated; retreated. Ever more desperately, she hammered on the door. But their hands went up, she felt things hitting her back—not very hard things, or if they were hard, the impact broke them. One hit her head. She put her hand up and came away with it sticky, with fragments of something—like eggshells, she thought bemusedly. Eggshells?

"You can't get away forever. We'll get you in the end, slag bucket. If not now, later," she heard, as the door opened.

"Flora! What are you up to? Whatever's this?" Jo's voice changed from anger to concern within a sentence. She waved her fist at the masked figures. She always had had a voice big enough to raise the dead; for once she used it, bellowing after the fleeing girls, "I'll give you trick-or-treat," so loudly, the young stockbroker next door looked out to see what was going on.

"Eggs," said Flora, removing her coat, determined not

to weep. She was shaking all over. "All over my back. They threw eggs at me, Mum. They threw eggs!"

"Yobs," said Aunt Jo. "I don't care who they are, what age they are. Yobs. Hooligans. I tell you, Flora, this trick-or-treating nonsense's getting out of hand. I'll give them *eggs*."

Only Louise, looking at Flora's egg-matted hair, her bespattered coat, at the fragments of eggshell, the messy trails of white and yolk on the door, across the doorstep, felt relieved, if anything. Marilyn had said she'd much worse things up her sleeves than eggs. Well, if she hadn't used them, maybe after all it was just talk. For what could three of them do, in the end? Lisa and Jacki were poor little things, really, Louise realized suddenly, under Marilyn's thumb no less than she was.

Flora, of course, felt no such reassurance. Upstairs in the bedroom, a towel around her newly washed hair, she opened the curtains and peered out. Though there was no more sign of Marilyn, three other ghostly figures were knocking on a door across the street. One turned, looked up at her. Its round white mask, with black holes for eyes and mouth, reminded her for a moment of the death's head masks worn by Jacki and Lisa.

And perhaps it was this, finally, amid fright, amid shock, that helped Flora make up her mind. Not only must she stop trying to pretend to herself that nothing was happening. The time had come for her to start finding out why her mouth spoke words she did not remember learning, why her fingers played tunes she did not remember practicing. She was going to have to establish, once and for all, whether she really was or was not Penelope as well as Flora.

(

Chapter
Fourteen

Guy Fawkes Day, November 5, came five days after
Halloween. To the Worth family, Guy Fawkes Day meant
the Ravenscourt Park bonfire and fireworks. In
Hammersmith, fireworks were already being set off all
over. The bad-tempered old cat in Cardew Road was so
frightened by them, it refused to go out all week. It just
sat under the kitchen table and grumbled. At school,
Piloo told Flora that it was *exactly* the same in Calcutta,
during Diwali. She accepted, eagerly, the invitation to the
after-the-fireworks party that Aunt Jo and Uncle Frank
had held every year since the Ravenscourt Park display
had been started by Uncle Frank and his Boys' Club.

Though the local council had taken it over long since,
Uncle Frank still regarded the display as his; November 5

was one of the few days he came home early. He wouldn't miss the fireworks for the world, he said.

"I wish you would come home early more often," said Flora.

On the fifth of November, Flora opened the front door at half past five to find Mrs. Bannerjee waving from the Volvo, and Piloo standing on the doorstep looking fat. Mrs. Bannerjee had taken to heart Aunt Jo's instructions to wrap Piloo up warmly. Upstairs in Flora's bedroom, Piloo emerged from her outer shell of coat, scarf, jacket, and sweater, clad in a yellow silk shalwar khameez, Punjabi dress, looking glossy as a chestnut.

"By the way, Flora," she said, eyeing Flora's glass animals. "By the way, why do you have two of everything? It is just like the story of Noah's ark." But she was squeezing Flora's arm with such seeming affection, Flora was mollified despite herself. She had never thought she needed people to like her before. But she was glad that Piloo did. As she was also glad that Louise, too, seemed to like Piloo. Louise even seemed to envy her friend's yellow silk.

Aunt Jo and Uncle Frank told Piloo how nice she was looking. "Pity you girls can't wear clothes like that," said Uncle Frank, eyeing Flora's old jeans and Louise's carefully selected Day-Glo pink leggings.

"Pity you can't, Dad," said Flora. Uncle Frank had donned a sagging green sweater and an old tartan scarf for the occasion. Louise did not get her interest in clothes from him.

Walking down King Street toward Ravenscourt Park, half an hour or so after, Frank and Jo issued stern instructions for when the fireworks were over. Though they weren't expected to stick to the grown-ups in such a crowd, the girls were to meet them at Ravenscourt Park Station at eight thirty sharp, not a moment later. "You girls are to stick together, mind," Jo said. "I don't want any of you wandering around alone, make sure you don't."

"There's my girls," said Uncle Frank, hugging all three of them.

Louise had been silent the whole way down King Street. Now she hissed, "Why should I stay with them, why should I?" She hadn't been angry when they set out. But the sight of Piloo taking Flora's arm had made her feel jealous suddenly.

Frank and Jo went on ahead. The three girls followed them down the narrow passage that led from Ravenscourt Road. Beyond the passage a wide grass space opened. Stands selling food and drink had been set up along an avenue of ornamental cherry trees and lime trees. The smell of popcorn and hamburgers extinguished the smells of cold and night. The beat of music, too, so filled Flora's head, that for a moment she felt quite dizzy with pleasure.

But then she saw them—Marilyn, Jacki and Lisa. At the same instant Louise saw Tracy Ann walking the other way, and disregarding her parents' instructions, ran after her, calling and waving. Piloo and Flora were on their own.

Flora pulled desperately at Piloo's arm to make her turn back. But Piloo took no notice and now, anyway, it was too late. Marilyn had seen them. Again Flora tried to pull Piloo away—in vain. Marilyn, clutching something in a shopping bag, was blocking their way. Behind her stood Jacki and Lisa, all three of them grinning. While

Flora stared back in horror, Piloo smiled uncertainly, as though she even thought they might be friends of Flora's.

But these weren't friends of Flora's. Far from it.

"Well," said Marilyn, "who've we got here then?" Where've you been all this time, bastard? Is it your Paki friend kept you away? Hullo, Paki," addressing a bemused Piloo, who did not seem to have understood the insult. "Hullo," she said uncertainly, smiling one of her polite smiles, Flora noticed. "Oh *hullo*," replied Marilyn, mimicking Piloo's accent, and making both her friends giggle, sycophantically.

"So, bastard, you've taken up with curry eaters," Marilyn went on. "When they go back to where they came from, are you going with them? Good riddance."

"Good riddance," echoed Jacki and Lisa.

Marilyn advanced closer. Piloo no longer seemed to think she was a friend. Pulling at Flora's coat, she whispered urgently, "Let's go, Flora."

"Not so fast, Paki," said Marilyn, taking Piloo by the arm. "Not so fast." Reaching out a hand she pulled off Piloo's hat, just the way, weeks back, she'd pulled off Flora's beret. "You won't need this back in Pakiland," she said. "It's hot where you're goin', in Pakiland." All her attention and that of her cronies was on Piloo. None of them, for once, took any notice of Flora. Piloo was trying to reach Marilyn's long arm, her hat, she was crying, "Give it back to me. Please give it back." Even here Piloo did not forget to say please, Flora noticed. Dropping Piloo's arm, she made a grab for the hat herself—got it— seized Piloo again.

"Come on, Piloo," she hissed, tugging at her. "Come on, run." And Piloo came. She ran, they both did. In the dark, among all the people it was not difficult to lose their tormentors. Yet still they could hear behind them, viperlike, the voices hissing, "Just you wait, Paki. Just you wait, bastard."

What had Marilyn got in her shopping bag, Flora wondered apprehensively? More eggs? She hoped not. But they were safe for now. The crowd was stirring, shifting, walking to and fro; thickening toward the center of the grassy space. It was almost time for the fireworks. Surrounded by people, Flora and Piloo, too, came to a halt. Flora handed Piloo back her hat.

"What very unpleasant girls," remarked Piloo, putting it on. "And why did they attack us, Flora? By the way, in London, is bastard often a term of abuse among schoolgirls?"

Shaking her head, Flora tried to speak. But her words were lost in the first uprush of fireworks. Red and green and white stars made an opening, followed by three loud bangs heralding sheets of golden rain so brilliant that they swallowed up the orange tinge of the light-filled city sky.

Though Flora could not help enjoying the display that followed, she did not enjoy it as much as usual. What could Piloo be thinking after all that abuse, she wondered. Racist abuse, Uncle Frank would call it. How she wished her uncle had been there to stop it. He was her father, after all—the nearest thing she had to a father. But he was not there. And as for Piloo, whenever Flora turned to look at her, Piloo's eyes were on the sky. Her expression was as calm as ever.

"Oh, don't you love fireworks, Flora?" she urged, to Flora's amazement.

Surrounded by people wrapped in scarves and thick coats, barely visible in the darkness, they were standing, Flora suddenly realized, at a place not far from the temporary wooden fence, behind which stood a huge pile of wood and other junk, otherwise known as the Guy Fawkes bonfire. Though the fireworks display was still only half done, she saw dark figures applying burning torches to the bottom of the bonfire. The flames they lit flared up quickly, soared boldly skyward. The smell of them obliterated for the moment the marvelous—so Flora thought—almost animal smell of the spent fireworks. All around them now, cheeks were glowing, eyes gleaming in the brilliance of firelight. Flora, keeping an anxious eye open for Marilyn, was thankful not to find her.

When she turned her attention back to the bonfire she saw that the flames had reached as high as the guy sitting on top of the bonfire. People were cheering. Most years Flora would have cheered with them. But this year, suddenly, she found herself feeling sorry for the Guy Fawkes dummy. Hearing a pounding behind her on the raised track of the subway as a Piccadilly train rushed past toward the city, she imagined that it was somehow coming to his rescue. But in a moment it was gone up the track, toward Hammersmith. And the guy caught fire, anyway, whatever she had wanted.

At that very moment, just next to where she and Piloo were standing, a man swung a small girl onto his shoulders. Flora heard the child laughing; looking up she saw the small face take on a rosy glow from the firelight. And as she did so, it was as if, suddenly, she herself, Flora, was in the child's place on the man's shoulders, looking down. Not so much now, though; in another time, another place.

In that other time she could not remember whether she actually sat on someone's shoulders, or whether she was just high up. She only knew a father held her tight. Not Uncle Frank, of course; not even her real father. Who then? *Penelope's* father?

There were other differences from that time, too. Then she had looked down on the heads of men mostly, while here the child looked down on women and children, too. Also it had been day then, not night, and the trees had been leafless, as in winter, or the end of winter, not autumn. Beyond the trees she remembered seeing a line of low hills rising. But in Hammersmith there was no line of low hills.

Football, thought Flora suddenly. That was it. That's what she and the man—her father—had come to watch. Furious, no-holds-barred football, "eat or be eaten" football. But why *football*, for goodness sake? Why did she think of football? Was it that all those crowds who sometimes shouted in her head reminded her of football? She remembered laying her head upon the father's shoulder, upon his head. Meanwhile the ball—which wasn't quite a ball, not the least round, to her memory—had flashed in and out of the seething mob of players. "Hold tight, Penelope," the father kept on saying. "Hold tight."

It was dark now. The flames of the bonfire were dying; the guy had vanished without a trace—burned, she supposed, to a cinder. Behind, from the railway tracks, came the rattle of a District Line train, heading for Ealing or Richmond. Flora no longer felt as if she was sitting on anyone's shoulder. She was standing with her friend, Piloo, hearing a further small waft of explosions. Above them fireworks were erupting again, one upon the other.

* * *

For all Marilyn's threats, Flora and Piloo would have been all right, probably, if they hadn't had to wait where they did, just outside the subway station, at Ravenscourt Park. The park gate nearest to the station having been closed, most people had gone to the next station up the line. There was no crowd here for them to hide in. Jo's instructions, anyway, forced them to stand outside the station, in the full glare of the lights. They were the first people Louise saw when she came walking down the road with Tracy Ann and some other friends.

Louise also saw, just ahead of her, Marilyn, Jacki and Lisa heading toward the station entrance. Flora and Piloo hadn't seen Marilyn yet. Louise watched to see what would happen when they did. Still more to see what would happen when Marilyn saw Flora.

And yet, just for the moment, it did not seem to have anything to do with her. Besides, didn't she sometimes want Flora, even now, to get her comeuppance—didn't she? So why should the sight of Marilyn advancing on her sister make her feel unhappy? Was it that she had spent so much of her life defending Flora that nothing else seemed right, let alone natural?

Louise looked around now, hoping to see her parents. Throwing eggs at front doors was one thing. But Marilyn would never confront parents, directly, she suspected; nor teachers, come to that, nor older girls. In general, Marilyn stuck to making trouble for juniors. But there was no sign of Louise's parents. On turning back, she could see no sign of Flora or Piloo, or of Marilyn, either, which was much more ominous.

"C'mon, Trace," she said to Tracy. Without bothering to explain, she ran ahead and in at the station entrance. To the left, just inside, were two public telephones, protected by plastic hoods. Marilyn had Flora and Piloo penned up between these plastic hoods and the end wall, alongside the iron gates which unfolded each night to close the station entrance.

Marilyn turned her head at this moment and looked behind her. Her face was not Marilyn's, though, not any longer. In those few minutes she'd donned the red-lipped devil mask. Jacki and Lisa, too, Louise saw, had put on their death's head masks. Backed right up into the corner, terrified, Flora and Piloo looked as if they were trying to shrink, to disappear right into the wall. But all the time their tormentors drew closer.

Louise could hear what Marilyn, Jacki and Lisa were chanting now. "Paki-lover, Paki-lover, Paki-lover," they hissed, over and over. And then—very low, but Louise had sharp ears and she was used to listening for Marilyn—"You know what happens to Pakis, don't you? You know what happens to Paki-lovers."

Piloo had pulled her scarf right across her face. Only her dark eyes could be seen, turning this way and that. As for Flora—Louise had never seen her cousin's face as ashen, not even during one of her headaches. The sight aroused in her all her old protective instincts. Besides, she wasn't her father's daughter for nothing; she hadn't lived all her life with his tirades against racism for nothing. If *he* came along now, of course, and heard what was going on, Marilyn and her friends would be mincemeat. But he did not come. And Louise, never a patient girl, could stand things no longer. Marching in at the station entrance, she turned sharp left, pushed Jacki and Lisa aside, and yanked Marilyn backward. The next moment she'd pulled the mask from Marilyn's face. She'd even thrown it on the ground and stamped on it, with a small twinge of regret because it had been a good mask; it really had been.

"Leave my sister alone, will you." she said. "If you don't, I'll get you." And she meant it. Jacki and Lisa both had their mouths open. Marilyn, her face strangely naked, just looked flummoxed. Louise almost laughed to see them. She didn't feel frightened in the least. It was as if, stamping on the mask, she'd stamped for the moment on her fear of Marilyn, too.

"Are you all right, Flor?" she asked. It was a long time since she called Flora "Flor," though she'd always used to. "Are you all right, Piloo? Get lost," she said, turning around once more to Marilyn. Marilyn glowered at her now, but stood her ground.

"Who's talking, Lulu?" she asked sweetly. "Who's talking?" She even took a step forward. Louise opened her mouth to say again, "Get lost, Marilyn." She was almost as big as Marilyn, she realized, though she was eighteen months younger. With her athlete's muscles she was almost certainly stronger than Marilyn. But at that moment Flora said, suddenly, "There's our mum, Louise, there's our dad."

Louise turned to find that Jo and Frank were indeed coming up the street. Marilyn, Jacki and Lisa left without another word. While Louise, suddenly as furious with Flora as she had been with Marilyn said, angrily, "That wasn't very bright, Flora. What's got into you, letting them bully you like that? Here, among all those people."

Piloo was unwinding her scarf from her face. "What very unpleasant girls," she said, smiling, her voice a bit high, though, a little brittle. "Do you know I've never had racist abuse before from anyone. That was racist abuse, wasn't it?"

"Yeah. You might say so," said Louise. "Best not to take any notice."

"How can you not take notice?" shouted Flora, her face as red suddenly as it had been white formerly. And to her own fury—it was almost unheard of—she burst into tears just like that, in front of everyone. Piloo then, not Louise, put an arm around Flora, with some difficulty, Louise noticed, given the amount of clothes she was wrapped up in. Because it seemed such a relief somehow, she burst out laughing at the sight. Jo and Frank arrived in time to see the other two, arms linked, staring at her indignantly.

Part Two

Chapter Fifteen

After Halloween, still more after Bonfire Night, Flora stopped trying to drive away her Penelope memories. Day by day, then, they grew more vivid, clearer.

They were not new memories entirely. They always had been there waiting for her to let them out. Now that she had stopped resisting them, each memory brought her more than just itself. It was like a fishhook, dangling down inside her mind, and pulling up out of it another memory. This memory in turn pulled up another. Between them they assembled whole days of a past life—places, people, smells, sounds, sensations—whether or not she wanted.

In one corner of the room with the bay window over-looking the garden, for instance, there had been a big white, tiled stove, reaching almost to the ceiling. On alternate tiles were little pictures drawn in blue. There were pictures of boats, of windmills, of men fishing, of men and women skating. Sitting on her bed in Cardew Road one day, Flora remembered standing there in front of them, on a polished wooden floor. It must have been in summer then, for the stove was cold, and she was tracing out these different pictures with her fingertips, the ones she could reach anyway. She was very small; not much more than five years old, probably. She heard a voice—a man's voice—Papa, of course—saying, "They are Dutch tiles, Penelope." And in her memory she felt herself lifted, so that she could inspect and touch the pictures higher up the way she'd been able to inspect and touch the ones lower down. There was one high picture, in particular, of a child and a man with a dog, she'd wanted to look at.

But it wasn't Penelope's father who lifted her, not this time. Papa was thin, while the man holding her up was so big and fat, she sank right into his belly. She could hear him breathing quite heavily, moreover. She saw his cheeks flush with effort beneath the fat white wig he always wore. Today the little bobtail at the back of the wig reminded her of the tail of her little dog, Tray.

The man with the bobtailed wig was Doctor Darwin, of course. So many memories of him had come to Flora that he must have been a friend of some kind, as well as her doctor. She had not been ill that day, for instance. Nor had she been the least bit poorly those other times when he'd taken her for a ride in his high-wheeled carriage. How high up she'd felt riding in the carriage with him. Higher than the quarters of the horse that drew the carriage, higher than the high garden fence. Beyond, in parkland dotted with tall trees, was a tear-shaped lake divided from another tear-shaped lake by a wooden bridge. "The fish ponds," Flora named them inside her head. Beyond the lakes the long valley ran toward a low line of hills.

The day Doctor Darwin had lifted her up to the stove, she remembered that there had been an argument of some kind. She did not know what it was about. Only that a woman—her mother?—had wanted to take her away. Flora had the impression this woman did not much like Doctor Darwin. But Mama—it must have been Mama—had lost the argument. When she left the room, Papa this time had lifted Penelope up. He had carried her out to the garden, talking over her head the while to Doctor Darwin. Then he had set her down on a path before a bed of plants. Doctor Darwin had bent and put his face to hers—his breath smelled of tobacco and peppermint and some things much less nice—and pointed out this plant and that, giving each name in turn, first in English, then Latin.

Flora remembered some of these names still. Reaching up to fetch her mother's little cabinet from the windowsill, she repeated them to herself. *Ilex Aquifolium*. And others. But that day she had repeated the names out loud to the two men. Fat Doctor Darwin had stammered badly, which did not stop him speaking very fast. She could hear him in her head now saying, "Well, B-b-brooke, we'll m-m-make a Linnaeus of your d-d-daughter yet."

Who was this Linnaeus, Flora wondered, now as then, even as she heard once more the father answer. "But then as you're always saying, Erasmus, it is just a matter of female education; for why should such knowledge, such talents, be the sole property of our gender? Her mother is teaching Penelope to play her instrument, to embroider. You and I together are teaching her botany, according to the principles of Linnaeus. And I, my good friend, am teaching her Latin. Apt scholar that she is, I vow she will surprise you one day soon with a recitation from Virgil."

Flora could not only hear her father's voice now, she could almost feel the gravel of the path under Penelope's delicately made slippers. She could feel the soft cloth of the dress she'd been wearing. The dress was white, its sash had been pink, she remembered, made of velvet, furry. How she had liked that pink velvet—much more than the blue or the green sashes she'd owned, also; they were made of a shinier material—satin? She remembered what her papa had been wearing, too, his black hat and fawn breeches. The ruffle on his shirt had tickled her arms while he carried her. He was wearing the same waistcoat that he'd worn in the picture Mr. Joseph Wright had painted of him. Was it the same picture, Flora wondered, as the one Jo had told her about in the Tate Gallery? If so, should she go and see it? Would she then find out who he was precisely? And thus who she—who Penelope—was?

Maybe Flora still wasn't quite ready for such thoughts. Immediately she let other memories drive them out; memories of someone whom she loved almost as much as she had loved her dear papa. She could hear Tray now, barking; Penelope's little white dog, the one that had died somehow. Tray had been alive that day, all right. He had come trotting after them, into the garden. As Penelope obediently repeated all the Latin names, he had thrust his cold nose right into her hand. She could feel his cold nose at this moment, hundreds—she thought it must be hundreds—of years later. She felt her hand damp, even cold, where the nose lay. And then came the feelings of grief because the dog would soon be dead; killed by another dog, she remembered suddenly. "Eat or be eaten" were the words that memory drew into her head, as usual, together with, in her mouth, a bitter, horrible taste of almonds.

All this made her cry, a little. She cried as Penelope first, weeping for her little white dog. But before long she found herself crying as herself, Flora, crying as she had not cried since she was five years old. For she too, like Penelope, had lost someone she had loved dearly. In her case she had lost her own mother.

Flora often sat on her bed after school these days. When she was not exploring her Penelope memories, she explored the cabinet and its contents. She set her fingers to tracing out the marquetry flowers decorating its top, the front of its little drawers. When she grew tired of that, she made patterns with the buttons that lived inside those drawers. She imagined her mother doing the same thing. She was sure her mother had played with the buttons too. Were any of the buttons old enough for Penelope to have played with them, she wondered. She licked a brass button as she did so. Even with her tongue she could tell it was a brass button, not a bone or china one. Perhaps Penelope licked the buttons once. Even if she had not, wasn't she licking them now, in some sense? Wasn't Flora's tongue now, in a way, Penelope's tongue?

What an odd thought; more than odd, scary. Yet it was not quite as scary as she would have expected. Maybe she was getting used to such ideas.

Louise entered the room sometimes when Flora was playing with the buttons. But she never tried to hide them from Louise now, the way she might have hidden them a little while back. And once or twice Louise came and perched beside Flora, on Flora's bed, and made her own patterns with them. Her patterns were quite different from the patterns made by Flora. She made circles and diamonds, even labyrinths of buttons, mixing them all up, brass with bone, with wood, with cloth, with mock diamond ones. Flora never mixed her buttons up. Her buttons marched sternly with their proper fellows, two by two. Except for the brass ones, they *could* all march two by two. There were six bone buttons, four wooden ones, four mock diamond buttons, eight ones covered with cloth. But there were only five of the tarnished brass buttons.

Louise made use of the solitary button in her patterns. She'd set it at the center, for instance. Flora did not know why the single button should upset her patterns so, but it did. Often she left the fifth brass button in its drawer. But she could never forget about it altogether—the very thought of it made her feel lonely. How stupid she was, to mind about a single button; but she did mind.

People had begun to notice that Flora and Piloo were becoming inseparable. At school they'd started calling them Flora/Piloo, or even the terrible twins, just as Louise and Flora had been called in primary school. Out of school they saw each other too. By now Aunt Jo and Mrs.

Bannerjee had met, inspected, and approved of one another.

"Too much money for her own good," pronounced Aunt Jo of Piloo's mother, balancing this at once by, "but surprisingly sensible, all things considered, she knows what's what, Flora." Mrs. Bannerjee, equally approving, called Aunt Jo "the salt of old England," according to Piloo. Flora had a vision of Aunt Jo being shaken out over London, like salt from a shaker. It felt right for Aunt Jo.

As for Mrs. Bannerjee, she seemed delighted that her daughter had made friends with someone from such a nice "down to the ground family" as she put it. Indeed it was she who suggested the arrangement that had Piloo, one afternoon each week, going home after school with Flora, doing her homework alongside Flora, having tea with the Worth family. While on another day Flora went to Queen's Mansions, to the Bannerjees' apartment, sat in Piloo's big room to do her homework, and had tea afterward with the Bannerjees. Mr. Bannerjee, a shorter man even than Uncle Frank, much older looking than Piloo's mother, joined them sometimes but not often. Usually he came in much too late to do so. He must, Flora thought, work as hard as her Uncle Frank.

Mrs. Bannerjee no longer felt obliged to provide Flora with such dainties as cucumber sandwiches. Sometimes she made Indian snacks: samosa, bhajis and so forth, or rice cooked with vegetables and spices. If Mr. Bannerjee was not at home, she even let them eat in the kitchen, although she giggled a little over this. It would not do, she said, but for what she called Flora and Piloo's "intimate" friendship.

When Mrs. Bannerjee sat in the sitting room reading

or writing letters, Flora would look anxiously at the piano. But, to her relief, though Piloo often teased Flora by pretending she was going to open it, she never did. Remembering being Penelope was one thing, Flora thought; doing the things Penelope had learned was something else. She had no desire to discover if there were any more Penelope tunes lurking in her—Flora's—fingers.

((

Chapter Sixteen

On Saturday mornings, Flora never saw Piloo. Saturday was the day the Bannerjee family went to the Hindu temple. After the half-term holiday Flora continued going to the dry-cleaning shop with Aunt Jo on Saturdays, just as she always had.

The first Saturday after Guy Fawkes night, Kathy wasn't there. In her place sat unfriendly Vida, who never smiled at Flora, never said a word. Vida was like that; Kathy had often assured Flora she was all right really. Vida had a hard life, she would add, mysteriously.

Today, however, Vida was not just unfriendly; she edged away from Flora. At the same time, whenever Flora turned around she had the impression that Vida had been staring at her, and that, like some startled creature, she had only this moment looked away. Sometimes Vida seemed more than startled. Raising her upper lip, she showed her teeth, the way a horse does when it is frightened. The right word for Vida's expression *was* "frightened," Flora thought. But why should Vida be frightened of *her*, Flora? What was the sense in that?

She did not like it. The next week, she was so thankful to find Kathy sitting in the window as usual, she forgot about being seen by Marilyn. She plonked her books on the sewing table and sat down beside Kathy in the old way.

"Decided we good enough for you, Flora, have you?" Kathy said, picking up Flora's Latin book. "You learning Greek these days, Flora?" she added. The way she grinned at Flora, though, made it obvious she knew it was Latin really.

"Give us a break will you, Kathy, *please*," said Flora, grinning back.

At the coffee break, though, when Flora drank tea with Kathy in the cramped little office at the back of the cleaning workshop, Kathy asked, "Well, then, girl, what's all this being about? You going to tell me?"

"What do you mean, Kathy?" Flora said suspiciously.

"You know what I mean, girl," Kathy said. "You know just what I mean. You want to make me say it?"

"Yes," Flora said, trying to be cold enough to put Kathy off the question, but not so cold as to put Kathy off her.

"Then I say it," said Kathy, smiling, as if she knew just what Flora was about. "Reincarnation, that's what I'm saying. You and that little girl. All that."

"I suppose Aunt Jo's been telling you," Flora said.

"Don't give me that, girl. Of course she tell me. You' aunt love you, Flora. She been worried. It don't worry me, but that Vida, she frightened to stitches about it. She say being it unlucky, don't want to come nowhere near you. You' aunt not saying it unlucky, of course, but she don't like to think you hiding it all from her. No she don't, Flora."

Well that explained Vida, thought Flora, with relief. But Aunt Jo talking about her to Vida and Kathy was another matter. Of course she and Aunt Jo didn't talk much these days. Flora had Piloo to talk to now. She also knew that if she and Jo did talk, she'd be asked more about Penelope. And she didn't want to talk to Aunt Jo about Penelope.

"You shouldn't listen to Aunt Jo," she said angrily. "It's a silly idea. She's talking nonsense."

"Is she then, Flora?" Kathy asked.

"Don't *you* think she is talking nonsense, Kathy?"

"What's it matter what I being thinking, girl?" asked Kathy.

"It can't be right," said Flora. "I mean, there's nothing to prove it; it doesn't make any sense. Just because my second name is Penelope, it doesn't mean I'm that Penelope also. It's stupid, Kathy."

Kathy said nothing.

"She died, Kathy. Penelope, I mean. That Penelope."

"Being worse things than dying, Flora girl," Kathy said.

"Would you want some dead person with your name in your head, Kathy, would you want to be reborn as her?"

"I would not," said Kathy. "But then I'm not so lucky as you, Flora. Being no little girl with my name in the past I come from. You' aunt she tell me about you, girl, that different. Nice little thing, she, rich daddy's daughter, name same as one of yours, two hundred years later. You don't think any of my people called Katherine way back, do you, Flora? Don't you know better than that, with all your education? Didn't you know little girls from my people, my tribe, were snatched away from their mammies. Names like Katherine weren't being their names, not the ones they born with, names like Katherine being given 'em by the people took them. By the slavers, Flora. Or maybe the slave owners, later. If I was a little girl from that many years back you know what I'd be remembering, Flora? I'd be remembering a slave ship and chains and being branded like cattle. You being glad of what you got, Flora."

Flora looked at her for a moment. "People aren't just reborn as their ancestors, Kathy," she said, hesitantly. "They can be reborn as anyone, my Indian friend, Piloo, says. I could be the reincarnation of one of your ancestors; you could be the reincarnation of one of mine."

"But I'm not being one, Flora, am I, not that I know of?" Kathy said. "And it seems to me from what your aunty saying, that you being the reincarnation of one of you' ancestors, not mine."

"But I don't know if Penelope *is* my ancestor," Flora said. And it was true, she wasn't sure of it yet, even though, given them all being called Penelope, it was hard not to think she might be.

Now too, reflecting on what Kathy had said, about being stolen from Africa, she remembered, for the first time, someone else she had known as Penelope. She could not think why she had not remembered him before. She had liked him so very much.

She met him only at the artist's house. During every sitting while he was painting her portrait, the elderly painter would put down his brushes after a while and say, "How about a small collation for my little miss?" And then a very small boy in a turban, whose skin had been the color of Kathy's, had brought Penelope a cup of hot chocolate and macaroons in a silver dish. His name was Joseph, Flora remembered. Sometimes he had stayed to play games with her, to keep her amused while the painter worked. He had seemed to enjoy the games as much as she did. He also seemed to like the hot chocolate and macaroons she shared with him.

Had Joseph come to England in a slave ship? Flora wondered. Had his flesh, too, been branded under his silk jacket and waistcoat, his satin breeches? He'd worn white stockings, she remembered, and buckled shoes. He'd smiled at her, always. He hadn't looked unhappy. But that didn't mean to say he hadn't been. Maybe at night, instead of sleeping, he cried as bitterly for his family as Penelope wept for Tray, or Flora for the loss of her mother.

Chapter
Seventeen

If Flora wondered why Marilyn, Jacki and Lisa had left her alone lately, Louise did not wonder. She knew why. After Guy Fawkes Day, she had dreaded going back to school. Despite her defeat of Marilyn, she kept seeing the devil look in Marilyn's blue eyes. She remembered the way Marilyn took locks of her fair hair in her hands sometimes, and drew them across her eyes like curtains before saying something nasty.

Even when she fell asleep, she dreamed of Marilyn. On Monday she contemplated not going to school at all. But it was a cold, wet morning; if she didn't go to school where *would* she go? And besides, she had a discus and javelin coaching session at four o'clock. Louise was determined she'd not let Marilyn keep her from that.

She need not have worried, as it turned out. She saw no sign of Marilyn from one end of the day to the other. And though she did bump into Jacki and Lisa on her way to the gym, they appeared as disconcerted at seeing her as she was at seeing them.

"Hullo," she said heartily, deciding to jump straight in. "I haven't seen Marilyn all day. Where is she?"

Jacki looked at Lisa, and Lisa at Jacki. Neither looked at Louise for a moment. Jacki shrugged then; immediately so did Lisa.

"Who knows, Lulu," said short plump Jacki.

"Who cares," said skinny Lisa, her nose red, as usual, her tights wrinkled, as if there wasn't enough flesh to fill them.

"The kind of trouble Marilyn's in these days she could be anywhere," added Jacki. But she didn't explain further. The look she gave Louise, however, might almost have contained a smile. But Louise had no more chance to find out where this was leading because the sports teacher, Mr. Wilcox, put his head out of the gym door to ask her, crossly, why she was still not changed. (It was in fact a good five minutes before the time Louise had arranged to meet him, but Mr. Wilcox was like that.)

Louise was to practice the swing of her discus throwing this session. She thought she'd be much too distracted to do well. In fact, the distraction seemed to help. Less worried than usual about getting the movement right, she did it perfectly at least once for the first time. It felt good, too, the swing of her body around and back again; it felt as easy as dancing.

"You *are* coming on, Louise," Mr. Wilcox said. "I'll have to see what I can do about coming over on Saturday mornings, so we can work on it a bit more."

* * *

Marilyn was not at school next day, either, or at least Louise did not see her. Nor did she talk to Jacki and Lisa again, though they smiled at her from a distance. Some of her classmates smiled at her, too. For once Louise did not feel a complete outsider. Her athletics helped. Louise sometimes went to practice with a girl called Angie Janes, and Angie Janes seemed to have told one or two people how good Louise was. It also helped that her chief tormentors, Keith New and Peter Blackston, had been passing Ravenscourt Park Station at the very moment she'd yanked Marilyn back, and that they had spread the news gleefully around the class.

Maybe not having Flora with her at this new school had been more of a problem than Louise realized. Maybe without Flora she'd felt much less confident than usual about her ability to make new friends. But now Louise did start to make friends.

Aunt Jo watched these developments with approval. At the same time she went on reflecting on her theories of reincarnation, aided and abetted by Piloo's mother, to whom she had confided the whole thing. Flora, to her horror—and fury—heard them discussing it over coffee. It was time they learned more about Flora's other self, Jo was thinking. If nothing else she owed it to Flora's mother. She remembered her friend with the usual pang of grief, followed by the usual sense of exasperation.

It was the least she could do, she thought, to launch Flora on the world with a good deal more sense than had been given her mother. What had *her* mother, Flora's grandmother, been like? Pen's own descriptions of the lady had merely shocked Jo at the time. "That dreadful old snob" was one she remembered. On other occasions, mysteriously, Pen had referred to her mother as "the fat white woman that nobody loves."

Jo had written to Pen's mother after Pen's death. But she had never received any answer. Since, on her deathbed, Flora's mother had made her swear to bring Flora up, Jo was not sorry about hearing nothing. She'd only written because she thought that Pen's mother had a right to learn her daughter's fate, no matter what she was like. When no answer came to her letter she had left it at that. Lately, however, the mysterious goings-on with Flora had set her to wondering once again whether she ought to try to contact her grandmother. Not least, she thought that Flora, too, had the right to know who her grandmother was.

What would Flora really like? she wondered. But she didn't want to add to Flora's confusion by asking her straight out. These days, anyway, Flora never gave her the chance to ask such questions. All Jo knew, or suspected, was that finding out about Penelope might be a means of finding out who Flora was.

In the end, Flora must find the truth for herself, Jo thought. The trip she planned to the Tate Gallery to see the portrait that had made Flora shout out, "Papa, Papa," was a beginning only. It was a brave beginning, nonetheless. Investigating Flora's family was one thing. What it might lead to was something else. Not least, she feared that it might lead to their family losing Flora altogether.

☾

Chapter
Eighteen

The visit to the Tate took place the Sunday after Flora had her conversation with Kathy. Jo put on her best coat and wore lipstick. She didn't wear lipstick very often; Flora wished she wouldn't wear it now. But when they met Piloo, as agreed, outside Hammersmith Station, Piloo's mother cried, "Don't you look nice, Josephine." (She was the only person, ever, to Flora's knowledge, who had called her Aunt Jo "Josephine"—since, that is, she'd agreed to stop calling her "Mrs. Worth.") "You always look nice, Geeta," Jo responded.

Piloo had been keen to join this outing. Piloo's mother had been even keener. She was most upset, she told them, that some visitors from India had turned up at the last minute to prevent her from coming. Leaning out of her car window, taking no notice of the cars behind honking at her to move on, she urged them all to bring her back postcards. Flora, meanwhile, had her suspicions about this trip. She was growing increasingly apprehensive.

Louise was also uneasy. She wouldn't have come, she thought, if she could have found something better to do this Sunday. Tracy Ann's mother never took her family to museums and galleries. Jo only did it, Louise thought resentfully, because of Flora's mother. Because Pen used to go to galleries and museums.

Today, though, they had come to see one picture only. From the central hall of the museum Jo turned sharp left into the rooms showing eighteenth-century paintings. The floors of the central hall had been made of marble. In these side rooms, their footsteps echoed on wooden floorboards with a sound familiar to Flora from two centuries ago. Floors these days were usually covered in carpets, or linoleum, or some variety of plastic; footsteps sounded quite different. But in Penelope's house. . . .

Stopping to gaze at a portrait of two little girls in yellow chasing a butterfly, she closed her eyes, tightly. She saw a wide hallway, its polished wooden boards quite bare of covering. Rising up from it was an uncarpeted staircase, with carved wooden balustrades. Down this came running the tall man Penelope called Papa, his footsteps making that same wooden clatter. A girl in a pink print dress and white cap had been holding Penelope's hand. But the man seized it from her. Out he and Penelope went, out into the sunshine, across the gravel, across the lawn. They went through a gate in the fence and over the high ornamental bridge you could just see from the window, to look at the fish in the fish pond. "My carp," Penelope's papa always called them. When bread was scattered upon the water, the great golden fish surfaced from the murky depths in much the same way as the memories of being Penelope surfaced two hundred years later in Flora's head.

Flora did not know if she was relieved or annoyed to be jerked suddenly out of such memories by a voice saying, "Come along, Flora." Jo's voice, definitely not a memory, definitely of now, was urging them out of this gallery and into the next. Louise could not imagine why they were in such a hurry. Flora knew, though. She had guessed what her aunt was up to from the start. Not that Aunt Jo seemed ready to admit it. She kept her red lips together, and when Flora looked across at her, she did not meet her eyes. Even now Flora considered turning, running back the other way.

The third gallery, too, had dark wooden walls and a high ceiling, as well as a wooden floor. Here at last, Aunt Jo found what she was looking for and came to a halt. Peering closely at the little gold disk that named the painter and his subject, she said, "That's it. That's *it*." "Sir Brooke Boothby, Bt," Flora read, bending to the gold disk in her turn. "By Joseph Wright. 1784."

Not that she needed to read it. She scarcely even needed to look at the painting. It wasn't that she remembered it as Flora. Last time she came here, she'd only been three, after all. But she remembered it as Penelope. The painting was absolutely her dear papa; at the same time absolutely not him. For how could something flat upon a wall be the same as a living breathing person?

Her father was a tall man, it seemed to her. But you could not tell how tall he was in the picture. In real life Penelope had never seen her papa lying down. In particular she had not seen him lying on the grass, though she had seen him bent very low, peering at flowers on the ground through his magnifying glass. "Look, Penelope," he would say, making her bend down beside him: "Look." And then, through the lens of the magnifying glass, he'd show her clearly all the parts of the flower: calyx, pistil, stamen. She'd been able to name them long before she was five years old.

What does "Bt" mean, Flora wondered, standing in the Tate Gallery that November day so many years later. Not that she intended to ask. Louise, meanwhile, peered at the white label on the wall beside the picture that announced that Penelope's father was "a minor poet, from Ashbourne, in Derbyshire." She demanded, disgustedly, "What's he lying like that for? It does look stupid."

"He looks very romantic," said Piloo. "And I like his hat. Don't you like his hat, Flora?"

But Flora still said nothing. Memories were stirring in her, not only of that broad-brimmed black hat, but of all the clothes the man was wearing. Except that she did not remember seeing him wear gloves, the way he did in the picture.

What a pity, she thought, that men don't wear clothes like that these days. Uncle Frank never wore any kind of suit unless he had to. She could not imagine him, though, taking to such coats and breeches, let alone wide-brimmed hats. It was just as well, probably; Uncle Frank was quite fat, as well as short.

Of course Doctor Darwin had been a great deal fatter,

and very ugly, his face not only broad, with several chins, but pitted with pock marks. And of course he'd worn breeches, black ones, with white stockings, Flora remembered. But he'd worn a big skirted coat on top, covering his big belly. Maybe if Uncle Frank were to wear such a coat he'd look all right, she thought, staring at the picture of her—Penelope's—father. He had a biggish nose, she saw, and a wide mouth; in his white curled wig he looked mild as a lamb and not the least bit ugly.

Aunt Jo said, "Your mother had blue eyes, Flora. Blue eyes just like that."

Louise said, "Why's he got a book? You couldn't read, lying like that. And you'd think he'd've crushed all those plants."

The meticulously painted detail of the plants interested Flora, suddenly. She leaned nearer and nearer the picture in order to see more clearly the heart-shaped leaves of the plants on the right-hand side. Pushing on the red ropes meant to keep visitors to the gallery back, she repeated under her breath a Latin name—"*Caltha Palustris.*" She did not hear Aunt Jo saying, "Careful, Flora. Don't get too close." When she felt a tap on her shoulder, she was as startled as if the dreamy-looking man in the picture had jumped out at her saying "boo."

She turned, reluctantly, to find a uniformed attendant shaking his finger at her.

"Careful, Miss," he said. "Keep back, please. If you don't mind. What do you think the rope's for?" Flora stared at him blankly. She wanted to protest, "But of course I can look at the picture, of course I can, it's my father, my papa." But she was twelve years old now, not three. So she contented herself with glaring at him, then moved her feet, ostentatiously, another three inches into the room, but no further.

"That was very rude of you, Flora," Jo said, when the man in uniform had gone. "The poor gent's only doing his job." "But," said Flora, "But . . ." Torn between a desire to express the injustice and an unwillingness to explain her behavior to her aunt, she could say nothing.

"Is everyone but me these days quite nuts, bonkers?" Louise asked the room at large. Flora opened her mouth once more, only to shut it again on hearing Piloo say, smiling and pointing to the man in the picture, "You know, Flora, don't you think the shape of your nose is very similar to that man's? Anyone would think he was your ancestor, they really would."

Aunt Jo thought it was quite time they left this gallery. She led them into another "to look for *my* picture," she said. By "her" picture, it turned out, she meant the original of her wedding present that hung on the wall of the sitting room; the picture of Isaac Newton plotting the world with a pair of compasses. And there the picture was, in a glass case showing the books *Songs of Innocence* and *Songs of Experience*, and next to another picture of a man measuring the world. This much more furious-looking figure, leaning down from a big cloud, was God himself, not Sir Isaac Newton. Flora took one look at him and started to shake.

For the second time that afternoon, she became, for a moment, Penelope again. On a damp gray October afternoon, her hand in her papa's, she was walking down the gravel path that led between an alley of hawthorn trees to the ornamental bridge spanning the Henmore Brook. The gravel shone wet beneath her feet, sodden brown hawthorn leaves were clinging to her shoes. She remembered pulling on her father's hand, as Doctor Darwin, more loudly than ever, stated that, in his not-so-humble opinion, the world wasn't measured by an old man sitting on a cloud. "Th-th-there's n-no such p-p-personage, no such G-g-god. Our w-w-world, our uni-v-v-verse is m-m-m-made, B-brooke, as I always s-s-say by the p-process of 'eat or b-b-be eaten.'"

Her papa had looked at Penelope, Flora remembered. "If you are not careful, Erasmus," he said, smiling, "you will infect my little daughter with your atheistical opinions. And how then shall I placate her mother?" Penelope herself, though, hadn't been worried about the possibility of being so infected. Doctor Darwin was always saying he didn't believe in God. His words couldn't make her shudder, one bit. But they made Flora shudder now, two centuries later. They made her remember all over again the terrible things that could happen. The terrible thing, in particular, that Penelope had seen happen to her little dog Tray.

"EAT OR B-B-BE EATEN," she repeated to herself, even mimicking the stammer. It was the stammer that reminded her at last that the phrase was, always had been, Doctor Darwin's. It reminded her that she—Penelope— had come in the end to hate Doctor Darwin. In just the same way—and at the same time—as she had come to hate the taste of almonds.

Piloo, meanwhile, was peering into the glass case, at *Songs of Innocence* and *Songs of Experience*. "Look, Flora," she cried. "Look. Here's 'Tiger tiger, burning bright.'"

But Flora did not want to look at "Tiger tiger." Her

head was pounding. And after one glance at her face, Jo marched them all downstairs to the basement floor to have a cup of tea and a cake each in the gallery cafe.

If Flora hoped to be allowed to forget Penelope, for today at least, she was disappointed. Her headache abated. As soon as she'd seen the color come back into Flora's cheeks, Jo decided that their seeing the portrait of Penelope's father had made this the right moment to go into the whole matter.

Still worse, in Flora's view, having said, "Ashbourne was where your mother came from, Flora," Jo added, "Just like . . ." She hesitated only for a moment before stating directly, "Just like Penelope's . . ." Then, worst of all, "*Your* father, Flora."

"So what?" asked Flora. And seeing Piloo's shocked look at her using such a tone to address her mother, she scowled at Piloo also. "So what if she did come from Ashbourne? What difference does it make?"

Aunt Jo pushed on relentlessly. "Your mother's name was Boothby, isn't that interesting, Flora?"

This time Flora objected so loudly that people at the next table turned and stared at her. "But it wasn't," she almost screamed. "My mother's name was Jebb. That was *my* name."

"I know, Flora. I know." Jo paused a minute, sighed. "All the same, love, she did tell me once it was really Boothby. That Jebb was just the name she used. I wasn't sure I believed her then—she did tell dreadful lies, sometimes, your mum. But seeing that picture now, well to be honest, I'm not so sure. And if you are Penelope's reincarnation . . ."

Her voice trailed away. Flora noted the lipstick marks on the cup she was holding. Why's she saying all this, in front of Louise and Piloo? she wondered again, angrily. Then, forgetting the presence of the other two, she found herself asking quietly rather than angrily, indeed almost pleadingly, the question that had bothered her all along. "If I am someone's reincarnation, Aunt Jo, if I know who I was in a past life, how come everyone doesn't?"

Aunt Jo did not answer. Flora, her voice more nervous than ever, hurried on. "I mean, Piloo believes everyone gets reincarnated as someone else—that's in Hinduism," she explained, noticing Louise, meanwhile, cramming an eclair into her mouth. Piloo, however, was leaning forward, encouragingly, her cup of tea stopped halfway to her mouth.

"Well then," she continued, "why doesn't everyone remember things about their previous lives? Why don't you, Aunt Jo? Why don't Louise and Piloo? Why's it just me has to?"

Aunt Jo started hunting for something in her handbag. She brought out her lipstick to Flora's horror, looked at it thoughtfully, then put it back. Louise, on the other hand, swallowed her eclair very fast, and emerged from it shouting loudly enough to make the people at the next table again turn around and stare at them. "I'm not anyone's reincarnation. I am *not*. Count me right out of it, Flora. *Yuck*."

Flora looked at Piloo. Piloo said, "Yes, of course, Flora, yes of course I believe I have been reincarnated. It is in my religion to believe it. But I believe also—I know that not many people know who they were in a past life, the way you do, Flora."

How unfair life was, thought Flora, gazing at the bewildered-looking Piloo. Because there was herself, Flora, who had no belief in such things, experiencing them, whereas Piloo, who believed in them, did not. It's my mother's fault, making my second name Penelope, she decided. It's all my mother's fault.

The way Piloo and Louise proceeded to take things over from that moment on first surprised then increasingly annoyed Flora. Piloo began it. On and on she went. "What about Ashbourne? Where *is* Derbyshire?" she asked. Then, "What about the Boothby family? What's 'Bt' stand for?" When Aunt Jo told her that "Bt" meant "Baronet," she said, "You mean you have a lord in your family, Flora? My goodness me!"

"My goodness me, Flora," said Louise, mockingly, "You mean I'm sharing a bedroom with someone descended from a lord? My goodness me!"

Louise had pretended not to be interested up till now. Yet she had not been able to help noticing that Piloo, for all her talk of research and libraries, knew a good deal less than Louise did about how to get going on such research. She didn't know about computer terminals, for instance; weren't there computers in her school, Louise wondered. There were plenty of them in Louise's school. Louise's class had been taught to use the library terminal in almost the first week of term. The second week, having been given a history project, they'd been taken off to the public library and shown how to use its system.

Some of Louise's class had grumbled about it. But not Louise. She had taken to computers like a duck to water. She knew exactly how to set about researching Penelope. She leaned across the table and said scornfully, "It's easy, you know. All you have to do is go to the library terminal and access it; you know, feed in the key word, whatever you want books about, and get on line. Then get the file up. It's easy. Easy as pie."

Her companions looked at her as if she'd begun suddenly talking Greek, or Double Dutch.

"Don't they teach you anything except Latin in your fancy school?" asked Louise, triumphantly. "On line. Means get in the catalog. You know. On a computer. Latin's mega useless," she added, scornfully. It all so cheered her, she found herself prepared, for the first time, to give attention—much attention even—to the business of Penelope's reincarnation in Flora.

Piloo, of course, defended Latin. But only briefly. Then she set about finding out from Louise how to use a library computer; in particular how to use it to track down books about Ashbourne. Soon her friend and her sister were so deep in discussion, Flora began to feel that she might just as well go home.

"Thanks very much, Louise and Piloo," she said, at last, angrily, "for turning Penelope—*me*—into your next school project. Thanks a *million*."

As for Aunt Jo, even though she was the reason for them sitting here in the first place, she too now, suddenly, seemed to have had more than enough. She got to her feet, and asked irritably, even sharply, why they were taking so long over their tea. Mrs. Bannerjee would be thinking that they'd kidnapped Piloo. What's got into her, Flora wondered. But she refused to acknowledge it might be the same thing that was getting into her. If her aunt *did* share her uncertainties—her half-wanting, half-not-wanting to find out where Flora's mother had come from—Flora preferred not to know.

☾

Chapter
Nineteen

Louise came away from the visit to the Tate Gallery, her head stuffed full of plans for learning more about Penelope and the Boothby family; full of confidence, too, that she knew just how to set about it.

Computers, however, weren't the only things Louise had learned about this term. Being unpopular had taught her plenty. Perhaps that was why she found herself thinking about Marilyn so often, as well as about Penelope.

She kept remembering those books that Piloo had showed her in a glass case—*Songs of Innocence* and *Songs of Experience*. Innocence, she thought, meant not knowing much about sex or anything else, for that matter. Like little children—Penelope for instance; or like Flora and Piloo, come to that, outside books. Wet behind the ears, Louise thought them. It must be that school they went to.

Experience, on the other hand, could mean knowing more than was good for you; so Louise's mother always said. Like Marilyn, for instance, to judge by the rumors that were going around.

These days Marilyn did not come to school very often, and even when she did come she appeared both pale and quiet. Her unmistakable laughter was never heard any longer echoing down the hall. One week Louise noticed what looked like a large bruise on Marilyn's left cheek. Hadn't Jacki told her that Marilyn's stepfather hit her sometimes? To judge by the look Louise saw in Marilyn's eyes, experience must have its drawbacks.

On the rare occasions she did bump into Louise, Marilyn would sometimes say things like, "My, who's getting beefy these days, Lulu. Anyone would think you were aiming at being a female Frank Bruno." But on other occasions she would act as if she wanted Louise to be her friend. Once she asked Louise to come around to her apartment again to play computer games. She even made it clear that she hadn't invited Jacki and Lisa. Though anything suggested by Marilyn still sounded threatening, Louise had the feeling this invitation wasn't a threat—that this time Marilyn meant it. She did not accept her offer, all the same. Though she admired Marilyn's mask-making skills, she still pitied her rather than liked her.

* * *

Research on Penelope occupied Louise more and more now. Her class had been given another history project. They'd been allowed to choose a subject for themselves from a long list. Though Penelope, of course, was not on the list, the social studies teacher had been so pleased by Louise's enthusiasm that he had let her choose the Boothby family to study. Her project was called "A Derbyshire Family in the Late Eighteenth Century."

Louise didn't say anything about this to Flora. She and Piloo went to the library together, Flora having refused to. It was Piloo who passed on to Flora what they'd found out; Flora seemed to mind less being told such things by Piloo—or perhaps even if she did mind, Piloo was too caught up by enthusiasm to notice.

Flora was not as uninterested as she pretended. She went so far as to think that having Piloo and Louise do all her work for her had its uses. A few days after the trip to the Tate, she even asked Jo for the picture of Penelope. At first she thought of putting it on the one spare bit of wall space on her side of the bedroom. But if she did that, she realized, Louise could also look at it. She wanted to keep some part of Penelope to herself.

She leaned Penelope's picture face to the wall therefore. Only when she was alone in her room did she turn the picture around and lie on her bed looking at her.

Apart from the oversize cap, light dress and dark sash, Penelope wore a kind of scarf wrapped crosswise around her chest, overlapping her sash somewhat. She sat hunched, her mittened hands and arms crossed in her lap.

In time Flora began remembering, dimly, a story her mother had told her long ago. The little girl in the picture had been friends with a famous painter, her mother said. She'd run away from home one day, no one knew where she'd got to, until her old nurse suggested she might have gone to see the painter. Sure enough, Penelope's mother had found her daughter asleep on an armchair in the painter's studio.

Was it that day or another—the story hadn't been very clear—that the painter said to the little girl, "I'm going to paint a picture of you, Penelope."

"No you are not," the little girl said, dumping herself down on a low stool, crossing her arms, hunching herself up, and scowling at him.

"Oh yes I am, Penelope," said the painter. "I'm going to paint you just like that."

And so he did, thought Flora, looking at the picture of the hunched-up Penelope, wondering as she did so how her mother knew that story. Had *her* mother told her? The sash Penelope was wearing when she was painted was a blue sash, she remembered. A dark blue; not a light one. Also, though in the picture the little girl sat before a group of trees, she hadn't been sitting in any park or garden while the painter painted her. She'd been sitting indoors, in his wooden-walled studio.

Little by little, Flora began to remember more about the painter. Standing behind his easel, his long-handled palette in one hand, his paintbrush in the other, he'd kept on looking between Penelope and his canvas. His brushes were made of camel hair, he'd told her. Once he'd drawn a little picture of a camel with a hump on its back to show her what a camel looked like, and more than once he'd let her touch the brushes, stroke the camel hair. Had the hair felt so soft on a camel's back? she wondered. Sometimes he had lifted her up and let her transfer small blobs of paint from brush to canvas. She remembered the floppy velvet cap the painter wore on his head in place of a wig, and the black patch that covered one of his eyes.

She remembered the mother's reproachful voice, how she'd burst into tears the day she'd found the lost Penelope in the painter's studio. Flora grew indignant with Penelope's indignation. "I didn't run away," she protested, in her high Penelope voice. "I came to see my friend, Sir Painter."

Time in the present was also passing. But Flora was almost too preoccupied to notice.

Of course, she had not altogether forgotten about Christmas. Every year up till now she would have already started to get excited. This year, till the afternoon she came in from school to smell the sweet smell of pre-Christmas cooking, she felt not the slightest flicker of anticipation.

There were hot smells and cold smells. The hot smell came from the still-warm oven, from the still-warm cake sitting on a wire tray, very big and rich and dark. Flora almost couldn't resist digging a little piece out of the beautiful brown crust. "Now then, Flora," Aunt Jo warned her. "Don't you dare." Just the same, Flora thought, smiling back at her, as in any other year. The cold smells came from the big yellow bowl sitting in the middle of the table, full of uncooked Christmas pudding, enough for all the smaller bowls stacked alongside. Aunt Jo never made just one pudding.

Nor had she ever been a tidy cook. Bags of sugar, packages of dried fruit, half-used bottles of brandy and port—there was always a lot of brandy and port in her puddings—still covered the table. Empty eggshells were heaped beside a plate of ten-penny pieces ready for the biggest pudding of all, the one to be eaten at Christmas.

"Do you want to stir the pudding and make a wish now, Flora?" Aunt Jo asked. "Or do you want to wait for Louise?"

Flora hesitated; then "Now," she said firmly, advancing on the pudding bowl.

It wasn't like mixing food, she thought, plunging the spoon into the uncooked pudding, apart from the smell, of course, the very pleasantly bittersweet smell of all that brandy and port. It was more like builders' work; like mixing concrete—yellowish, brownish concrete, studded with raisins and nuts, very stiff, very heavy, despite the eggs and port and brandy. She had to take two hands to the spoon.

"What are you going to wish for, Flora?" Aunt Jo asked her.

Gripping the long wooden spoon, Flora considered the problem. She wished for so many things; some of them trivial—like getting 10 out of 10 for the English essay she'd just handed in—some not the least trivial. She wanted to wish Penelope a longer life, for instance. What a waste of a wish that would be, thought Flora; how could you stop something happening that had happened two hundred years ago already? Just the same she wished that she could prevent Penelope from dying; or at least prevent her from dying so young. She wished it in just the same way that, reading stories in which she knew the bad things that were to happen, she found herself willing the characters to turn back before it was too late. (Stay with Heathcliff, Cathy. Mr. Toad, if you keep driving like that you're going to end up in prison.) In just the same way she used to wish herself back in time, sometimes, to the day of her mother's accident. She used to imagine herself shouting, "Look out, Mum, *don't*. There's a bus coming." In vain.

Closing her eyes, she began once more to stir the mixture. Had Penelope ever stirred Christmas pudding? she wondered. Though the smell evoked no particular Penelope memory, it confused her. By the time Louise came home, she couldn't remember if she'd made a wish or not; and if she had, which wish.

Louise took the matter of stirring the pudding much more lightly. Flinging her pack down so hard that her books fell out, she gave the pudding one casual stir, with her eyes shut. Then she burst out, "I just went to the library, Flora, and do you know what I found? A whole book about Sir Joshua Reynolds, the painter who painted the picture of Penelope. It was quite an old book, and it had a story about her running away from home and going to the painter's studio. And about her not wanting to be painted, and sitting down just the way she's sitting in your picture."

Flora thought, but *I* know that story. Staring at Louise, she was at first quite shocked. The next moment, however, joy overcame her. Because Penelope was hers, after all. Anything Louise could tell her, about Penelope at least, she, Flora, was almost certain to know already. She didn't have to look up her life, Penelope's life, in books.

"What's the matter with you? You look like a cat got the cream," Louise said.

"Do I?" said Flora.

"Yes, you do, Flora, what got into you, my ducks?" said Aunt Jo.

"Nothing much," Flora said, still smiling. "Can we phone Piloo?" she added. "I bet Piloo's never stirred a Christmas pudding."

"I bet Piloo," said Louise, "will just think its an ever-so-quaint English custom. Or her mum will. Do we want it to be a quaint English custom?" But Aunt Jo said eagerly, "Yes, why not? And ask Mrs. Bannerjee to come too."

"Mum really likes Mrs. Bannerjee, doesn't she?" said Louise when she and Flora were lying in bed that night.

"She likes lots of people," said Flora. "She likes Kathy and Betty at work."

"But they don't make her giggle," said Louise. "When she's with Mrs. Bannerjee, she goes on just like you do with Piloo. It's weird, Flora."

"Not quite like us. A bit different. They are grown up," said Flora.

"*Supposed* to be grown up," said Louise. "But I'm beginning to wonder what that means exactly," she added, thinking of her would-be friend Marilyn.

Flora fell asleep wondering if her mother and Jo had giggled together the way Jo and Mrs. Bannerjee did. Hoping that they had. But next day the news came that pushed all such things, even Penelope, to the back of her mind.

☾

Chapter
Twenty

Only Flora's feelings about it were quite unmixed. Aunt Jo's feelings were mixed from the beginning, she made that clear. But then she had always believed, she said, in being honest with Flora. Even to Flora she couldn't pretend, she said, that she looked forward entirely to this extraordinary, not to say unheard-of event—the reappearance of Flora's father.

"Uncle Ray?" asked Louise. "You mean there really *is* an Uncle Ray? I gave up believing in him before I gave up believing in Santa Claus. What's he want to come for, spoiling our Christmas?"

"Careful, Louise," said Flora. "That's my dad you're talking about." It was the first time in her life she'd been able to use such words. Casually. "My dad." She practiced saying it to herself. "My real dad."

Uncle Frank said to Aunt Jo, on the other hand, when Flora was out of earshot, "Well, I always did say 'Good riddance to bad rubbish,' about that one. Maybe I shouldn't have. Garbage all gets recycled these days. It looks like Ray's gone and got into the act."

The news had come by letter. "From Scotland, I think," Aunt Jo said, peering at the postmark. It didn't say much. Just something about an old soldier turning up again like a bad debt. And "How about killing the fatted calf for your prodigal brother, sister Josephine." It didn't even say what day he was proposing to come. Only a scribbled postscript, which Jo could hardly read, referred to Flora. He made no mention of Flora's mother. Aunt Jo had sent him news of her death, care of Poste Restante, Liverpool, soon after it happened.

Once, Aunt Jo had given Flora a picture of her father. It stayed at the back of her underwear drawer, in an envelope, along with a picture of her mother. But from the day the postcard came, till January the first, when her father went away again, she kept the envelope under her pillow.

The picture she had of her father was bigger than the one of her mother. He was wearing an army uniform. He'd been in the army for five years, Aunt Jo told Flora. The picture had been taken just before he left, just before he met Flora's mother. About two years before I was born, Flora worked out, but did not say. The man staring boldly out at her from the photograph had very thick eyebrows above dark brown eyes. He looked like someone in a magazine, she thought, not like a living person.

Maybe it was the uniform he was wearing; the way the shine on the brass buttons matched the shine of his slicked-down hair. Maybe it was because he looked so tall when in fact, according to Jo, he'd not been particularly tall, except compared to Flora's mother. To Flora he looked as unreal as Penelope's father looked lounging on the grass in gloves and dun-colored suit, in his gold-framed portrait. As unreal as the picture of Jo and Frank on their wedding day that sat on the mantelpiece downstairs and that had never looked to Flora like Aunt Jo and Uncle Frank.

The photo of Flora's mother was not posed and neat like that of Flora's father. It was only a snapshot, taken at Jo's wedding, and rather fuzzy. Very skinny, she'd worn a pair of tight satin trousers and a pink Indian shirt topped by an embroidered waistcoat. She'd had beads braided into her long brown hair. The party, Aunt Jo said, had been going on for a long while by the time the picture was taken. A glass in her hand, and no shoes on her feet, Pen had been smiling up at someone. At Flora's father? Flora had always thought it must be. For it was the smile of someone who liked the person she was smiling at more than a little. Soppy, thought Flora severely. On the other hand she was glad her mother had liked her father. If he could make her mother smile so, she was sure she, Flora, was also going to like him. She wished he'd let them know what day he was coming, though. It was only three and a half weeks till Christmas; two weeks till the end of term. But they'd heard nothing more.

Flora spent every moment that she could spare making a special present for her father. The diary was all Mrs. Bannerjee's idea. "Every time your father has to write down some appointment, Flora," she said, "he will think of his clever daughter." Flora did not know if her father was the sort of man who made appointments. Mr. Bannerjee certainly did, but her father did not sound the least like Mr. Bannerjee. Nevertheless she loved Mrs. Bannerjee's suggestion. She loved it still more when Piloo's mother, seemingly as excited as Flora was, found some beautiful grainy paper, printed in gold and red, to bind the diary.

Flora did not tell anyone at home about the diary she was making at the Bannerjees' apartment. She told Mrs. Bannerjee and Piloo it was to be a secret between her and them, and they promised it would be. Every time Flora brought the diary out to work on, Mrs. Bannerjee put a finger to her lips and smiled, conspiratorially.

These days when Flora went to tea with Piloo, instead of doing her homework, she sat ruling black lines in the diary to make the days of the week. She drew little pictures to decorate each day. To decorate each new month she chose pictures from a pile offered her by Mrs. Bannerjee, showing Indian gods and rajahs and beautiful ladies in saris, or showing animals, like elephants, monkeys, birds or tigers.

Sometimes Mrs. Bannerjee said, "We are being so naughty, Flora, playing hooky like this. What about your homework? Do you promise me you are not skimping your homework?" And then Flora had to promise her she was doing the work at home. And so she was. But she was skimping it badly by her usual standards. "Oh Flora," said Miss Wainwright, among others. "What's happened to you? Your work's going right downhill."

"Flora was doing her Latin. Flora wasn't doing her Latin. That's imperfect all right. Anyone would think these days Flora was a human being," giggled Emma

Pelham to Ginny Black. Flora no longer cared the least what they thought of her. She giggled back.

If Flora was skimping her homework for Christmas, Louise, on the other hand, was skimping Christmas for her research into the Boothby family. She hadn't yet decided on, let alone bought, a single present. Her history teacher was as pleased with her as her athletics teacher these days. By now it wasn't just pleasure in computers that drove Louise's interest in the history of Penelope's family; she was interested in the subject for its own sake. Mr. Marple, her teacher, took to bringing her books from a library he belonged to. Often, when she came home, she reported her discoveries to her mother and Flora.

Louise had learned from a book about Ashbourne, for instance, of Penelope's father's fondness for gardens. He had started a botanical society with someone called Doctor Darwin, she told them. He had improved his gardens, made fish ponds and other things. When Louise described the fish pond to her adopted sister, the carp swam up in Flora's head all over again, for a moment even displacing thoughts of Christmas. She hardly heard Louise go on to describe what good friends Doctor Darwin had been with Penelope's father. Penelope's father didn't feel so much like hers, now Flora was going to meet her own father.

Louise came home with more and more information about Doctor Darwin. Doctor Darwin had been so much more famous than Penelope's father that it was far easier, she said, to find out about him. Apart from being fat and having a stammer—here again Flora checked her memory, and felt her usual secret satisfaction that Louise could tell her nothing new—apart from being a doctor, he was also a poet, an inventor and a scientist. Louise was much more interested in his being a scientist than she was in his being a poet. Even when she discovered, to her disgust, that he wrote up scientific ideas *as* poems.

None of it especially interested Flora. She knew nothing about the doctor's scientific ideas, or so she thought. But then one evening Louise came out with something said by Doctor Darwin which Flora knew all too well. She had never realized, though, it had anything to do with his science.

Mrs. Bannerjee was ensconced at the kitchen table with Aunt Jo that day, drinking coffee. Flora and Piloo were leaning against the counter, eating cookies. Louise didn't even bother to take a cookie before bursting out that she'd found out only today that Doctor Erasmus Darwin was the grandfather of Charles Darwin; and that it was Charles Darwin who'd always been thought to have invented the theory of evolution.

"That's people being descended from monkeys rather than Adam and Eve," she added, helpfully. "Mr. Marple explained the whole thing. But the book says people have always got it wrong. It wasn't Charles Darwin who invented evolution. Doctor Erasmus Darwin invented it."

Mrs. Bannerjee knew all about Charles Darwin. She leaned forward and said brightly, "Yes, of course, Louise, here we have all that famous business about survival of the fittest in the deathly struggle for existence. Which is telling us that the strong will always be devouring the weak."

"Nature red in tooth and claw," said Aunt Jo. Almost

at the same moment, Flora repeated, hardly knowing she was going to, "The first law of creation is very simple, my dear Brooke. Eat or b-b-be eaten."

She hadn't said it very loudly. No one seemed to have heard—Louise, Mrs. Bannerjee, Piloo were all talking at once about the theory of evolution. But she had heard such ideas long before they had. And it was awful.

Flora had a dream that night. From it she awoke into what was not a dream, but a memory, a dream of snow. It was the kind of snow they had in Derbyshire, that she knew as Penelope, not the gray, instantly melting London snow she knew as Flora. Thick, picture-book snow, it ought to have evoked nice things, like snowmen and toboggans. But it did not. She awoke from the dream in a state of dread. And as she lay there, remembering, little by little, all—or most of it—came back.

The snow had not been so deep that day that the roads were impassable. Doctor Darwin had come in his high-wheeled carriage to tend someone who was sick in the house. Just who had been sick, Flora—Penelope—could not remember. She could remember Doctor Darwin sitting down at the table—a long way back from it because of the bulk of his stomach—to eat the food provided for him when he came; the same kind of food, always. There were dishes of fresh fruit (apples, she remembered, in winter) and of preserved fruit—Portugal plums, that day. There was Stilton cheese and clotted cream, and a little plate of Naples biscuits. As usual he ate heartily, not ceasing to talk, waving the knife he used to pare the fruit or dig chunks of cheese out of the whole Stilton sitting on the table before him; flourishing the silver spoon with which he supped up the cream.

He argued against religion as usual. Penelope's mama pursed her lips disapprovingly when, also as usual, he mocked not just a belief in God, but belief in a world to come, in the likelihood of reincarnation.

"M-m-man has b-b-but five g-g-gates of knowledge, the f-f-five senses. As for the existence of a s-s-soul, who c-c-can know anything a-b-bout it," Doctor Darwin declared, waving his knife at Penelope's father, sitting across the table from him, not arguing for once, just smiling ironically. Beads of sweat edged Doctor Darwin's eyeglasses; his face was redder than ever. Every now and then his stammer caused him to spit little bits of apple or Portugal plum or gobbets of cream across the table. And when he was done with eating he mopped his brow with a big handkerchief he took out of the pocket in the skirt of his big black coat, wiped his mouth on his napkin, patted his huge stomach as if to congratulate it on its efforts and said, "And n-n-now little m-m-mistress, it is quite t-t-time, we gave some healthy exerc-c-cise to one of your f-f-five s-s-senses. D-d-do you think m-m-maybe I've got s-s-something f-f-for you?"

Expectantly Penelope watched him feeling in the same pocket in which he'd only just replaced his handkerchief. But his hand came out empty.

"Deuce t-t-t-take it," he said. "I th-th-think I l-l-l-left them in the s-s-sulky. S-s-something must be d-d-done about that."

He'd sent for his coat then; also Penelope's coat. He'd wrapped her up in it himself, while her nurse, fussing a little, had pulled on her overshoes.

"N-n-nonsense, n-n-nonsense," he'd said when the nurse protested how cold it was outside. "The f-f-fresh air will d-do the little m-m-maid g-g-good." The big front door had been flung open and out they went into the cold air, so cold their breath smoked before them.

The light was low already. The doctor pulled out his big watch from his waistcoat pocket and, looking at the yellowish sky above the low line of snow-covered hills on the far side of the valley, muttered more to himself than to Penelope that he must make haste to be home in Derby before dark. It would snow much more tonight.

The doctor's carriage, the sulky, stood on the far side of the gravel sweep. It was a very high carriage, with a hood, now closed against the weather, and a seat that held only one—at least only one Doctor Darwin. John the footman had already fetched the doctor's big dog from the kitchen, where it had been fed and kept warm; it waited for him under the carriage. Doctor Darwin only brought this dog with him on the days on which he did not have to travel too far from Derby. It ran along behind the carriage, behind the big water bucket and the bag of hay hung there for the doctor's horse, its long legs covering the miles as easily as the still longer legs of the horse covered them.

The dog was taller than Penelope. Even though it had always been friendly enough she gave it an apprehensive glance as the doctor opened the door of the carriage and lifted her up. Flora still remembered the smell inside the carriage, two hundred years later. A smell of man. Of leather. Also of peppermints, tobacco, horse, ink. And that day, of course, it smelled of cold.

The smell of ink came from a kind of pocket hung in

front of the driver, in which there was not only a large bottle of ink but also pens, a sheaf of scribbled-on paper, and some eating utensils—a knife, a fork, a spoon. On the floor on the far side was a pile of books. But none of this was what they had come for. The big hamper by Penelope's feet was more to the point. Doctor Darwin always carried this hamper. From it came goodies of one kind and another, goodies otherwise known as Doctor Darwin's collations, brought to stop him from going hungry during his travels.

There was not much in the hamper today; Doctor Darwin had not expected to be away from home for long. But no matter how long or short his journey the hamper always contained sweetmeats. Grunting as he stood on the step of the carriage, he bent forward to the hamper, and extracted first some barbary drops, and then a handful of burnt almonds. Penelope did not much like barbary drops, but burnt almonds were another matter. Watched by Doctor Darwin and by her father now, she crammed them into her mouth, laughing with pleasure.

It was the last time the taste of almonds gave her pleasure. At the very moment her mouth was full of it, she'd heard Tray's familiar yelp. She looked out of the carriage over Doctor Darwin's bewigged head to see him come running out of the house, barking with excitement.

Tray skidded to a halt immediately below them. His forefeet dug into the ground, his fluffy white tail waving, he continued his frenzied barking, little high notes amid deeper ones. Penelope heard the other dog then, suddenly. She heard it growl before she saw it. Almost immediately she did see it. She saw its teeth, within its snarling mouth. She saw it, before her very eyes, pick up the little dog, in that mouth, those teeth, saw it shake Tray, ferociously.

You could not exactly say the big dog bit Tray's head off; it did not quite bite his head off. But it might just as well have done. She saw the white of the bone amid the blood; a yellow white against the snow's innocent whiteness, just as his white fur was gray compared to the snow's whiteness. The blood—Tray's life blood—was brilliantly red. But Tray was dead anyway, dead almost the moment she saw the jaws of the big dog open, heard Tray's yelp of terror, dying instantly to nothing.

Penelope stood quite rigid for a moment, choking on a bittersweet mush of burnt almonds. Then she began screaming so loudly she did not notice Doctor Darwin reach out an arm to clasp her. She hardly saw the men running and shouting below her, separating live dog from dead. Penelope's father had a hand on the carriage rail now, was pulling himself up—holding out a hand to take his screaming daughter.

Doctor Erasmus Darwin handed her down. He said, very coolly, "A p-p-perfect example of what I've always s-said, my d-d-dear Brooke. That in n-n-nature the strong devours the w-w-weak." Still now, Flora could hear the interest, the fascination in his voice, in the way he spoke, even as he comforted her, embraced her. "In m-m-mother nature," he went on, "It is a m-m-matter of eat or b-b-be eaten."

Thereafter, of course, he'd tried to comfort Penelope again. He had execrated his big dog, used his whip on it, execrated himself for owning such an animal, sworn to buy her another little dog Tray. In all these ways he'd shown himself distraught at having caused her such wretchedness. But still she could not, would not, forget the way Doctor Darwin had spoken; his tone, even amidst her sobs, of such keen, such burning interest. "Eat or b-b-be eaten."

Eat or be eaten, thought Flora. And of course in a way it was so. Look at Tray. But if he was right in *that* matter, he wasn't right about everything, was he, she thought in triumph and with anger. Not about souls; not about there being no souls, no world to come. No reincarnation. For here *is* Penelope's soul, in me; it must be. And this is the world to come, or at least one kind of world to come. Which means you don't—you didn't—know everything, Doctor Darwin—did you? Horrible Doctor Darwin, she thought. Serves you right.

☾

Chapter
Twenty-one

Flora had finished making her father's diary. She had
wrapped it, labeled it, made a card. Dutifully, but with
much less interest, she bought and wrapped presents for
the rest of her family. She also bought presents for Piloo
and Mrs. Bannerjee, who were so excited at the prospect of
spending Christmas in England that Aunt Jo invited them
to join the family for Christmas dinner. Sighing, Mrs.
Bannerjee refused the invitation. "If it had just been Piloo
and myself," she said. "But Mr. Bannerjee. . . . You know,
he is not a social person, Josephine. He is a person for his
family always, and that is enough." When she went on to
tell Aunt Jo how many Bannerjee aunts, uncles, cousins,
there were in Calcutta, Aunt Jo said, "With *that* many, he
might have a point, Geeta. It might be enough."

But as for Flora, all she thought of was the arrival of her father, day and night.

Aunt Jo tried to calm her down a little, to warn her. Ray could never be relied on, she pointed out. He'd still not even told them when he was planning to arrive. Maybe he wouldn't come. He was like that. The way she said this made Louise suspect she'd be thankful if he didn't come. But Flora wasn't listening either to the things Aunt Jo said, or the things she didn't. "Of course my dad will come," she said. "Of course he'll come."

The house was all ready for Christmas now. Alan, home from the university, spent most of the time out with his friends. There was holly along the pictures in the sitting room, cards strung up on the walls, and a Christmas tree masking Isaac Newton. Flora wondered if he would have approved. They didn't have Christmas trees in the eighteenth century, which meant Penelope wouldn't have known anything about Christmas trees either. What a shame.

Flora's father was going to have to sleep in the sitting room. His bedding, too, was ready for him days beforehand, Flora saw to that. But by Christmas Eve all they'd had from him was a card saying he'd got delayed, he had some business to finish. "Hmph," snorted Aunt Jo. "I can imagine what kind of business." And again she tried to warn Flora not to be too hopeful. And again Flora refused to listen.

And she was right not to; Ray did come. "Blowing in" was the right way to put it. Christmas Eve was a windy day and he left the front door open. All the paper chains Flora had put up in the hall to welcome him blew this way and that. One, suspended from the light fixture, slipped down, masking the mistletoe, draping itself around him.

"And so this must be my little girl," was almost the first thing Flora heard her father say. Only he said it to Louise, which just went to show, Louise said to her mother later, how stupid Uncle Ray was. How could he possibly think she was his little girl? For one thing, she wasn't little.

Though Ray was not a tall man, he looked much bigger than Flora expected, standing there in the narrow hall, draped in her homemade paper chain, and with his luggage—most of it in shopping bags—around him. Maybe it was because he'd grown fat. Or maybe he seemed so big because in her mind he'd only been a shadow up till now. Even with the scraped feel of her cheek where he'd kissed her after learning she, not Louise, was his daughter, she could hardly believe he was real. Any more than she could believe he belonged to her. The front door had been shut behind him. In the dim light of the hall, she stood staring at his tangled dark hair—he, her father, had long hair—at the solitary gold earring in his left ear. His faint but bulky shadow gleamed on the linoleum floor. His coat huddled around him, spattered with rain. He seemed like something blown in from the world outside. He did not seem like part of home.

And maybe he did not feel part of home, either. At tea in the kitchen, still wearing his outdoor coat, he did not even sit square to the table. He sat sideways, as if ready to flee any minute, Louise thought. Unlike Flora, she had no interest in finding her uncle pleasant, let alone liking him. She noted, quite coolly, his beer belly, the broken red veins on his cheeks. She noted the way his dark hair receded from his forehead, the way his gaze fled around the room, never lighting on anything for long; in particular never lighting for more than an instant on his daughter.

Flora, on the other hand, could not take her eyes off him. Only when he'd asked for and drunk two cans of beer did her father begin to relax. And having relaxed he became noisy. His laugh was much too big for their kitchen, Louise thought. But Flora smiled at the sound of her father's laugh; and her brother Alan laughed back. Uncle Ray made a fuss of him, man to man, passing him cans of beer as one drinker to another, winking at him, saying, "Now then, Alanman, you're a big boy now, drink up."

This did not fool Louise for one minute. She was an athlete, after all. Uncle Ray, she thought, was like someone at the beginning of a race, swiveling his eyes around at all the other competitors—any of them more likely to win than he was. He was a loser, she thought, if ever she saw one.

Ray slept late on Christmas morning. Alan would have liked to do the same; he'd gone to the pub with Uncle Ray the night before. But Flora and Louise would not let him. Ever since they ceased to believe in Santa Claus, the whole family had taken to opening their stockings together around the breakfast table, and it would not be the same, Louise said, without him.

"It serves you right, lad," Uncle Frank said, winking at Flora, "letting your Uncle Ray buy you all those drinks."

Flora, though, did not wink back at him. She did not want her adopted father making jokes about her real one. At this moment she did not want to have much to do with Uncle Frank at all. She didn't even want to like him.

Flora had made her father a stocking, as well as a present. She'd hoped he would get up and open his stocking with the rest of them. Yet now she didn't protest when Frank added briefly, "Best to let your father sleep."

Jo, too, nodded. Not until they'd finished breakfast did she say, "You can take your dad a cup of tea now, Flora, if you'd like to."

No answer came to Flora's knock at the sitting-room door. After a minute, doing her best not to spill the tea, she pushed it open and went inside, blinking in the gloom of the darkened room to get her bearings. It did not smell like their sitting room. It smelled of sleeping man for one thing. It smelled, just a little, of beer, and more than just a little of cigarettes—there was a heap of stubs in a saucer beside the bed. At the same time it smelled of pine needles from the Christmas tree. The brightly wrapped presents under it were still piled up, still ready to be opened, she saw, with a lift of excitement.

Her father was a hump under the blankets on the settee. He did not stir even when she set the cup down on the floor beside him. "Dad," she said. "Dad," trying the word out on him for size; the first time she had done so. Last night she had not dared. It seemed easier, somehow, with him asleep. And perhaps he even heard. For all at once, his eyes flew open, he stared up at her, blindly.

"It's all right, Dad. It's only me, Flora," she said. "I've brought you some tea." And at once, overcome with shyness, she fled, or tried to, tripping over some of the bags and parcels heaped on the floor, before she managed finally to get herself to the door.

In their family, they always opened their presents

around eleven o'clock. This year, even having to get Flora's father up first, they were in the sitting room by half-past eleven. The settee was turned back from bed to settee now, most of Uncle Ray's things out of sight.

He'd brightened up, somewhat. He insisted on his handing out his presents before the rest. All but one of the loosely wrapped packages lacked labels, Flora noticed. Inside were gifts of talcum powder, incense sticks and chocolates, as if he'd just gone out and bought a selection of things and wrapped them up without thinking. Her present was the exception. Not only was it larger than the rest; it was also the one with a label.

But Flora stopped smiling as soon as she opened the package. Staring up at her from between the torn wrappings was a doll; a huge Holly Hobbie™ doll. Only Flora's father seemed oblivious of the look on Flora's face as she gazed at the pink-faced, simpering-faced, fat-faced creature. Dressed in a pink, sprigged dress, its feet looked like fists, its sash was absurd and its eyelashes even absurder. Its huge mob cap was like the one worn by Penelope. The doll was altogether like a caricature of Penelope, she thought, dismayed. Anyone would think he'd done it on purpose. But of course he couldn't have, could he?

Flora's father was telling the room at large, now, "It cost a bit, man. But what the hell, nothing's too good for Flora, my long-lost daughter, I thought when I bought it. Nothing's too good for Flora."

"Thank you," Flora managed to say, at last. Not even "Thank you, Dad." Just "thank you." Wordlessly she handed him in her turn the present she'd made with such loving care—first the little stocking, one of her socks, in fact; then the appointment diary. What kind of appointments did *he* have? thought Louise cynically, when she saw Flora's secret at last.

All of them admired the book that Flora had made. As for Uncle Ray, staring from the diary to Flora and back as if he couldn't believe what he was seeing, he said, wonderingly, "You made it, Flora, you really made it, for me, for your long-lost, shameless, neglectful daddy? Man, man, man, what a daughter."

Flora didn't see much of her father over the next week, up till New Year's Eve. None of them did. The time he was home he spent asleep on the sofa, or in front of the television set. Now and then he winked at them; said he had business, he had to see a man about a dog; he was going to make our fortune, Flora, see if he didn't.

"Don't give me fortunes, Ray," Aunt Jo said, sharply. "I've heard it all before. But I've yet to see it."

On New Year's Eve at last, however, Flora found Ray alone in the sitting room, sitting on the settee, looking glum. "Come to cheer up your old dad, have you, Flora?" he asked her. He glanced at her then, and said, "You look like your mum, Flora, did you know?" And when she replied, hesitantly, "I've got a picture of her. Do you want to see it?" he told her he did; and she went to fetch it.

He stared at the photo of Flora's mother with her dazzled expression for a long time. At last he said, "Your mum, Flora, she was the most beautiful thing I ever saw. She was the best thing ever happened to me; her and her lovely fancy accent. Fancy *her*, falling in love with *me*. It was the worst thing I ever did in my life, walking out on her like that. Can't think why I did it. I couldn't imagine myself as a dad I suppose. We aren't all like your Aunt Jo, Flora girl, good at families and that. Seemed best just to go, let her get on with it. I knew Jo would look after her and you. And she did. But I missed Pennylope, your mum, Flora. How I did."

He pulled a cigarette out of the packet in his denim jacket and lit it. Flora saw his fingers trembling a little. And then she saw, she could hardly bear it, that the tears were running down his cheeks. Aunt Jo had always said it was the one thing about her father, that he'd really loved her mother. And she was glad. On the other hand, she thought, he couldn't love her, Flora. How little she had seen him, all week. She was almost in tears herself now, seeing him slide out of the room, still crying, not giving her so much as a second glance. A moment later she heard the bells on the Christmas decorations tinkling in the wind from outside, heard the front door slam. He's not like Uncle Frank, she thought, sadly. As for Penelope's father, he had scarcely let *his* daughter out of his sight. Her father wasn't like that papa at all.

The suitcase of dressing-up clothes from her mother stayed under Flora's bed now. Today, for some reason, straight after dinner, she lifted it onto her bed. Louise came into the room the moment Flora began pulling the clothes out. For a while they both tried clothes on, pirouetting in front of their small mirror to see what they looked like.

It was easier for Flora, of course. The clothes that had belonged to her mother fitted her—if they weren't too big—whereas they were mostly too small for Louise. "Hot pants, those used to be called," Louise said, looking almost envious as Flora, having pulled on the satin shorts and the scoop-necked purple T-shirt, added a tasseled shawl and an embroidered hat.

"You look great; *dudey,* Flora." As Flora peered in the mirror and paraded before her, Louise was thinking that her sister was becoming human at last; she'd never been interested before in the way she looked.

Piloo and Mrs. Bannerjee were coming over that day, for the first time since before Christmas. They brought presents wrapped in paper covered with bells and holly, and sounded disappointed with Christmas. At Indian festivals, Mrs. Bannerjee told Aunt Jo, everyone came on the streets, there was music and dancing, processions. But here everyone had stayed at home. It had not seemed like a proper festival.

They heard giggling in the hall then. Piloo had gone upstairs to find Louise and Flora, and now they were all on the other side of the door. A moment later they marched into the room. Piloo and Louise were swathed in shawls from the dressing-up suitcase, smelling of mothballs. But Flora was still wearing the satin hot pants. She had added a pair of ribbed black tights for warmth and the embroidered boots. Under the velvet cap, her long hair was threaded with little braids like those her mother used to wear—that was Piloo's idea.

Aunt Jo could not believe what she was seeing, or thought she was seeing in the glittering lights of the Christmas tree. She opened her mouth to tell Flora to go and change at once—she did not say Flora looked too much like her mother, but that was what she meant. But by this time Mrs. Bannerjee was saying how nice Flora looked. Moreover she chose that moment to start handing out their presents; which meant Aunt Jo had to go and fetch the presents prepared for her and Piloo. By the time she came back into the room, Flora and Louise were opening their holly- and bell-wrapped packages and it was all too late.

Mrs. Bannerjee and Piloo had given both Louise and Flora Punjabi dress; a pink shalwar khameez for Louise, a red one for Flora. Louise went off to try hers on at once. But when Mrs. Bannerjee said, "Flora looks so nice already, and I know what she looks like in Punjabi dress," Flora decided to keep on her mother's clothes.

She had forgotten all about her father; she blinked at him when, suddenly, he entered the room. After one glance at her, his eyes fled the other way, toward Piloo and her mother. Mrs. Bannerjee was wearing a sari, Piloo green Punjabi dress; their silks shimmered in the multi-colored light from the Christmas tree. After a moment his eyes fled back toward Flora.

"Pennylope," he said. "Pennylope, ——— it," using a swear word none of them were allowed to used in this house, not even Uncle Frank. "Pennylope. Come here, little love. Come to your big daddy . . ." But when he began advancing on Flora, arms out, pleadingly, she took fright, clutched for support at the nearest person, who happened to be Mrs. Bannerjee. Her father stopped dead, staring at them. Then he used another word no one was allowed to use in Uncle Frank's house. "Hullo, Mrs. Paki," he said. "How are you, Mrs. Paki? That's my daughter you got there, did you know that, Mrs. Paki?"

He paused a moment, looked around, but did not

seem to notice the horror on all their faces. "My lovely daughter," he went on. "What's my Flora doing, going to a Paki, when she's got her old dad, her darlin' long-lost old dad? Come to me, Flora, come to me, Pennylope . . ." He made one more step toward Mrs. Bannerjee. Flora, her hot face buried in the cool silk of Mrs. Bannerjee's sari, could feel her quivering. But still, standing alongside the Christmas tree, Mrs. Bannerjee didn't move a step, not even when Flora's father reached out a hand to take Flora from her.

Aunt Jo was also advancing now. Moving sideways slightly, to avoid her, Ray succeeded in missing Flora. He clutched at the Christmas tree instead. Several colored balls fell with thin tinkles to the floor. The fairy slipped from the top and slithered down a few branches. It startled him for a moment. And in that moment Aunt Jo took Flora in her arms. When Ray pleaded with her, "You let me have her, she's mine, my little Flora, my Pennylope," she shook her head.

"No, Ray," she said firmly. "That's more than enough, more than enough for one day. You just lay off." As if she was talking to Louise and Flora about something. Not talking to her own brother.

"It *is* more than enough," Ray said. "Tell Flora to take those clothes off, Jo, tell her to take them off this minute. What are you thinking of, letting Flora wear Pennylope's clothes? And letting all these Pakis into the house too."

He spoke to Flora now, directly. "Take them off, Flora. Just take those clothes *off*, will you."

But Flora wasn't thinking of clothes any longer, or, for once, of herself. She was thinking of the Bannerjees. She'd never forgive her father, never, she thought, for speaking to her friends like that. For the first time in her life she not only had friends, she found herself defending them. "No, I won't take them off, I've got a right to my mother's things. More than you have," she shouted, bursting into tears. "Piloo's my friend. Mrs. Bannerjee's my friend. They're much more my friends than you are."

Her father went out then, slamming first the sitting-room door behind him, then the front door, so hard that the whole house shook. Aunt Jo, Flora, Louise and the Bannerjees resumed their tea party; but it wasn't the same, and the Bannerjees went home early, though not without affectionate good-byes. Mrs. Bannerjee kissed Aunt Jo on the cheek and whispered, "Do not worry, Josephine, every family has its bad apple. Do not think it will alter my friendship for you. No Josephine, it won't."

"I should hope not, Geeta," Aunt Jo said with some of her usual tartness, kissing Mrs. Bannerjee back.

After this, neither Louise nor Flora had the heart to see the New Year in, though this year, for the first time, Aunt Jo had promised they could. Both fell asleep quite quickly, tired out. When they awoke, late at night, to hear shouting on the stairs—Uncle Ray must have come in drunk—Flora lay trembling thinking of all the horrible things she'd seen on television and in the papers, but never expected in her own home, with Aunt Jo and Uncle Frank to protect her. Louise, though, as usual, was thinking of Marilyn, wondering if this kind of thing, too, was what was meant by the word *experience*. If so, she could do without it. Poor Marilyn, in whose family, it was whispered, much worse things happened.

Next morning they woke, much later than usual, to find that Ray had gone, his belongings with him. All that was left for Flora was a scrawled note. "Thanks for the diary," it said. "Sorry about the fuss. You deserve a better dad, chicken. But don't you ever stop loving your lovely mum."

"Good riddance to bad rubbish," said Uncle Frank. "Bugger recycling." Later he took Flora aside, hugged her, said, "Don't worry, Florakins, you've got a dad all right, you've got me." The most he'd ever said to her on the subject; it made her cry all over again. But gratefully, if sadly.

Part Three

☾

Chapter
Twenty-two

After Christmas Louise began writing up the results of her research into the Boothby family and Doctor Darwin. Writing was harder work than researching; her enthusiasm cooled a bit. She was discouraged not in the least by her mother and sister's lack of interest in what she had to tell them. Aunt Jo, more often than not, would say, "Fancy, Louise," absentmindedly, and then go on to say how worried she was about Flora. While Flora herself merely nodded in the abstracted way of someone ticking off items on a list already in her possession: Doctor Darwin liked eating fruit and cream—tick; he invented his own carriage—tick; Sir Brooke Boothby spent a lot of money re-landscaping his park and garden—tick. And so on. At night, sometimes, she talked in her sleep, using a little high voice, which did not sound like her own. By day she'd look at Louise and say quite calmly, "I want to go to Ashbourne now, Louise. I want to go."

Around the middle of January, Louise came home from the library one afternoon, full of excitement. "Did you know, Flora," she cried, "Penelope's tomb is in the church at Ashbourne? It's made of white marble and Penelope—I mean the statue of Penelope—is lying asleep on it, carved by a sculptor called Sir Thomas Banks. It's famous, Flora."

But Flora merely looked at her and said, "It can't be very famous if you've only just found out about it, Louise." But then she shivered and fell silent. And when Louise said, "I'd like to see that, it'd be like—well you know, Flora, interesting—mega interesting," Flora shivered still more and stated, violently, "Well, I *wouldn't*."

"Well, I suppose it would be a bit like seeing your own tomb, Flora," suggested Louise cheerfully. "Creepy; just *creepy*." To which Flora replied, still more violently, "Of course not; of course it's not my tomb. Of course not."

For a few days she even stopped wanting to go to Ashbourne. At least when she was awake she did not want to go. At night, in her sleep, she cried out in her high Penelope voice, "Papa, Papa." And added, very clearly, to Louise's astonishment—*could* she be hearing right—was Penelope Boothby driving Flora quite crazy—"Take me to the football, Papa. I want to see the football."

The discovery Louise made a day or two later reassured her a little. As Penelope, Flora might well remember football. There *had* been football, if not the kind of football Louise's brother Alan supported. She wasn't mad, after all.

"It's special to Ashbourne, you see," Louise told Flora. "On Pancake Day and the one after every year since goodness know when. It's like everyone plays in it—all the men anyway. They play it over the whole town, and there's two teams, Uppards and Downards, that's men living above some stream on one side, and men living below it on the other. They all have dinner first; the game goes like from two o'clock till ten o'clock at night, and they use some special kind of football for it, and somebody important each year starts it off. It sounds really weird; but really exciting, Flora."

"It sounds historical to me," said Piloo, who was with them. "Don't you think it sounds historical, Louise?"

As for Flora, the memories crowded so furiously into her head she could not prevent herself speaking them out loud.

"That's it. That's how I remember Papa's holding me high up. The day of the football. Looking at all the men struggling to pick up the ball; they're allowed to pick up the ball, you see, in that kind of football. That year, he was the important person starting it; he threw the ball in. And then they all went running away with it. And then they all came running back. They ran right through the town and broke the windows of the wig shop. There was glass all over the street, and Papa said, 'This is no place for you, Penelope,' and took me home. Mama was angry with him for taking me at all, and they had an argument about it."

Flora paused for a moment. In her head she saw the thin arch of wood over the street, just beyond the wigmaker's shop. The wood was painted green and on it was written in big gold letters, which Penelope could read, little as she was: THE GREEN MAN.

"Is there something called like The Green Man in Ashbourne, Louise? Is there?" she asked her. "Do any of the books you've seen say that there is?"

Louise looked triumphant. "Of course I know," she said. "The Green Man's a pub in Ashbourne, right in the middle. It's where they start the football from; or used to."

After what had happened on New Year's Eve, Aunt Jo felt such shame at her brother Ray's behavior that, despite Geeta's assurances, she assumed her friendship with Mrs. Bannerjee was over. When school started again, Flora asked if she should go to tea with Piloo as usual on Wednesday, the day she always went. Aunt Jo said certainly not. Mrs. Bannerjee would not be expecting her.

But at school Piloo told her friend she was expected to tea, just the same. And when Flora, obedient to Aunt Jo, went home instead, Mrs. Bannerjee rang Aunt Jo and said—very politely—"This is all such rubbish, Josephine. We're much too good friends for *that* to make any difference." With Aunt Jo still saying nothing, Mrs. Bannerjee went on, still more insistently, "Wasn't I saying, Josephine, that in all families there are bad apples? In my family we are having a most dastardly nephew, he makes everyone very ashamed. I am only talking about him now, Josephine, just to show that all families are the same, so enough of this rubbish, please."

"Poor little Flora," Mrs. Bannerjee added. "Please be giving her a great big kiss from me, Josephine." And maybe it was this, the tenderness with which she spoke, that convinced Jo. When Mrs. Bannerjee invited her to coffee the very next day, early closing day at the shops, she accepted at once.

After that, in the Worth family, things continued just as before; or seemed to. Flora went to school, came home or went to Piloo's, did her homework. Did it properly, moreover—the school had no complaints. Jo had no complaints about Flora's behavior either. As for Penelope's reincarnation as Flora, she decided for the moment to let sleeping dogs lie.

Louise still hadn't told her mother about Flora's talking in her sleep. She hadn't told her about the football even. It wasn't Aunt Jo to whom Flora kept on and on, saying in Penelope's voice she had to go to Ashbourne.

Her mother was still worried about Flora, though, Louise could see. One day she found Jo sitting in the kitchen holding the Holly Hobbie doll, ripped open in places and filthy dirty. She'd found it stuffed into the trash can, her mother said. And then she added, sighing, she supposed it was fair enough; Flora had every reason to be angry with her father, and better she took it out on a doll than on any of them.

Next day, though, Louise heard her telling Mrs. Bannerjee about the doll. She heard them coming to the conclusion that maybe it wasn't just what had happened over Christmas, it was quite as much the time of year that ailed Flora. Mrs. Bannerjee said the English winter was making her feel a bit blue herself, if she was honest.

Kathy at the dry cleaners was much less certain that this was Flora's problem. Louise heard her talking to her mother about Flora when she called in at the dry cleaners on her way home from school one day. Afterward, while her mother was dealing with some customers, Kathy turned to Louise and whispered, "You look after that sister of yours, girl. She not too happy, I think. You get worse bellyache from bad memory than from too much dinner, I tell you, Louise."

As the weeks went by, however, Louise began to grow used to her disturbed nights. But then Flora's headaches started all over. And then, just after half-term, Flora played Piloo's piano.

Louise and Piloo both saw her doing it; Louise, too, was at the Bannerjees that day. Dazed, white, her expression trancelike, Flora sat down and played tune after tune—simple, easy little tunes, it is true, but still tunes. She played them beautifully, according to Mrs. Bannerjee, who claimed to have an ear for music. Flora took her hands off the keys at last, folded them demurely in her lap. Then she turned to Piloo and Louise with a smile that did not belong to Flora and said in the voice that Louise kept hearing at night, "Did I play well, Papa, did I?"

Next day, in the kitchen at Cardew Road, she cried out, so violently she startled everyone including herself, "I've got to go to Ashbourne, Aunt Jo, I've got to. It's time to go." Adding in that same high voice, "Isn't it time to go to Ashbourne? Is it not the time of year we always go to Ashbourne, Papa? Isn't it time to go and see the fishes?" Turning to Louise, she added, "I want to see the football, Papa, I want to see the football."

((

Chapter
Twenty-three

It was getting toward Shrove Tuesday. That was one reason Flora kept on thinking of the football.

She remembered her nurse telling her all about it— her nurse was an Ashbourne woman. She remembered John the footman telling her about it too; he was an Ashbourne man. Mama, though, said it was not suitable at all, the game was for rough, common men of the town, not for a little daughter of the landed gentry. Her father was to start the game this year in honor of his high position in society. As lord of the manor, it was natural his more lowly neighbors should ask him to inaugurate their revelries. But it was not for Penelope, his daughter, to attend them.

But Penelope did not agree. Imposing the same strong

will on her father that was now imposing itself on Flora and her family two hundred years later, she begged and begged to go. When Louise, hearing the ever more frantic beseeching from Flora's sleep, wondered if Penelope had taken Flora over entirely, she was not far wrong. As for Flora, she only knew that she wanted so badly to get to Ashbourne to see the football, she'd forgotten all her fear of finding Penelope's tomb. She had no strength left any longer to resist what Penelope wanted.

Aunt Jo by this time was thinking quite seriously of taking Flora to see another doctor. As for Shrove Tuesday and football, she wouldn't hear one word about it. Shrove Tuesday was a school day; so was Ash Wednesday, the second day of the football. Yes, she knew Flora must go to Ashbourne one day, to see where Penelope came from; to see where her mother most likely came from. But from what she could see of the football—from what Louise told her—that wouldn't be the day to go.

"*Drunk* men," she said, looking at Flora. "Best to keep out of the way of them, Flora. Best to keep well away." Much like what Penelope's mother had said, really, though phrased in the terms of quite different times. It was not the slightest use Louise asking, "So what? There's plenty of drunks in our street when Fulham's playing football at home." Nothing could sway her.

Penelope, though, was stronger than all of them. Louise guessed as much when she saw Flora's bank savings account book lying on Flora's bed.

"How much is the bus fare to Ashbourne, Flora?" she asked, very kindly. "What time does the bus go? You have looked up in the timetable how to get to Ashbourne, haven't you, Flora?"

But Flora had not. So now Louise looked it up for her. If they took the bus from Victoria Coach Station to Derby, she discovered, they could connect with a bus for Ashbourne. No hassle, as Louise put it. With luck, if they left home at the normal time for going to school—Aunt Jo, of course, had to assume they were going to school as usual—they'd be in Ashbourne by lunchtime. "Easy," said Louise. "We'll leave mum a note on the kitchen table. She'll find it when she gets home, and then she won't worry—she'll know exactly were we've got to."

She spoke with more confidence than she felt. In their family such behavior was unthinkable, really, or would have seemed so till lately. As for Flora, if she resented Louise's taking over arrangements, she didn't say. She was grateful, anyway, at the prospect of Louise keeping her company. Despite everything, she was scared of going to Ashbourne and for more than one reason. She was still more pleased when Piloo insisted she was not going to be left behind. Piloo, of course, had to work still harder to square her conscience. In India, as she was always telling them, you had to honor your parents; people would be shocked in India at the way that English girls behaved. But, on the other hand, she thought Mummyji would consider she ought to help look after Flora. She would ring her from Derby, explain things, tell her not to worry. Once that was all decided, Piloo worried no longer. She was sure she was doing the right thing.

Then all that remained was the journey to Ashbourne; on Ash Wednesday, in fact, rather than Shrove Tuesday. Louise said it would be a pity to miss the pancakes at home on Pancake Day. And besides, her mother, knowing what Flora wanted, might be watching a bit too carefully on Shrove Tuesday. So it was on Ash Wednesday they went, leaving home at the usual time, catching the 9:15 bus from Victoria to Derby. Flora clutched in her pocket, wrapped in several layers of tissue paper, the walnut shell from the little wooden cabinet—the shell hinged like a box and lined with green velvet—in which lay the two little teeth. Penelope's teeth?

The journey went without a hitch; they arrived in Ashbourne exactly as planned at lunchtime. The only thing that did not go according to plan was Piloo's phone call. Her mother was out; she had to leave the message on the answering machine. But if reaching Ashbourne was no problem, the same could not be said of what happened when they got there. Almost at once Louise's worst fears were realized. The crowd was far worse than they could have imagined. The mob of people that surrounded them the moment they stepped from the bus almost instantly swept them apart.

☾

Chapter
Twenty-four

One result of their losing one another was that, out of the three of them, only Flora saw the game start. Another was that although all three reached the Church of St. Oswald and Penelope's tomb, they reached it separately, not together.

It was Louise who got to the tomb first. That was why she missed the start of the game at the far end of town. As soon as she realized she'd lost the other two, she'd concluded that what Flora would be most likely to do—at least what *she* would be most likely do if *she* was Flora—would be to look for Penelope's tomb. She searched the skyline for a church spire and, having found one, headed toward it.

The first two doors she tried in the gray stone wall of

St. Oswald's Church were both locked. The third door lay within a big porch; the big iron latch was stiff, but it opened. She went inside, blinking in the gloom. Though it was hard to see much, it did not take her long to find the Boothby Chapel. Separated from the chancel by carved wooden screens, it contained tombs from end to end; in all of them, Louise assumed, with a feeling of awe, were the remains of people from whom Flora was descended. On each tomb, carved stone figures were lying on their backs, their hands folded across their bosoms, their feet pointing upward.

Penelope's small white marble tomb was in the farthest corner. But she wasn't lying on her back, she was curled up on her side like a real child. Except for the marble she might have been a real child, thought Louise, as, a little sad, even reluctant suddenly, she approached the tomb on tiptoe. Penelope lay on a white stone bed, on a white stone mattress. At one end was a white stone pillow, on which the little white girl laid her white stone head. Her feet were bare. The folds of her dress were gentle, like cloth; yet the cloth was stone also.

Louise had believed herself alone in the church till now. But suddenly a big man in a sagging tweed jacket and an ill-knitted, green scarf rose from behind the white marble of the tomb, brandishing a cleaning cloth, and proceeded to wash the little white stone body, almost tenderly, humming to himself as he did so. Louise could have sworn the tune he was humming was "Baa, Baa, Black Sheep."

In the gloom of the church he did not notice Louise at first, any more than she had noticed him. As soon as he did see her, he stopped washing the stone Penelope, reached a hand back, and pushed down a switch. The chapel around them sprang into harsh lights and shadow.

"Have you coom to see the famous tomb of Penelope Boothby?" the man asked Louise in a strong Derbyshire accent—at least it sounded strong to her, she was not used to Derbyshire voices. "Then you found t'right man to show you. I'm the verger here. I'm Penelope's guardian. I wash 'er every day, it's part of us duties. Such a bit of a thing, she was; died much younger than you, miss. And I can tell you how she died: meningitis, it was, what they called brain fever, in them days. Gives you dreadful headaches that does. They never got over it, her mam and dad—they never said now't more to each other after they left t'graveside. She blamed him, you see, for taking Penelope to watch t'football. It wor just after t'football she got ill, you see. She died. And it wor such a funeral, never wor such a funeral. Sky cried much as t'people, raining cats and dogs, it wor, on t'morning they buried her, all those years ago. Five little girls carried her coffin. Five little boys held umbrellas over t'small girls; only t'coffin got wet."

Much of all this Louise knew, as it happened. She knew about Penelope's funeral, for instance, about the five little girls and five little boys. She'd never told Flora. It would have felt like describing to her sister the details of her own funeral. Nor was she going to tell this man that she knew what he was telling her. She only wondered how to stop him talking. Outside the church, a great roar went up in the distance; the football game must have started. Where *was* Flora? she wondered, anxiously, as the noise of the game drew nearer.

Wringing out his cloth for the last time and draping

it neatly across a pillar, the verger jerked his head toward the nearest window. "There they go again," he said. "There they go again; crazy; every year it's t'same, crazy. In Penelope's time too, I daresay. Nothing better to do have they, ruffians all of them; not like t'gentry; not like this lot"—he jerked his head at the tombs all around him. But what use to them was being gentry now, thought Louise. Fancy tombs or not they were all dead, weren't they? In the end, gentry or ruffians, inside the church or out, winners or losers in the struggle for existence, it came to the same thing.

"Ta ta," she said to the crazy verger—he was crazy, wasn't he?—he was bending over Penelope now almost as if kissing her good night. Nuts, thought Louise, scornfully. Hurrying out of the church, she almost fell over a thin, rather bent, gray-haired woman, in a dark gray windbreaker, carrying an armful of dusters and a big tin of brass polish.

Piloo did not head for the church straightaway. She was not worried about being lost; she was sure she would find her friends eventually. *This* is more like a festival in India, she thought, as soon as the game started, seeing the mobs of people, the shouting men; *now* I can see the English know how to do it properly. Then she walked up into the town, looking around her with great interest. Consulting a copy of the town map that Louise had given her, she tried to identify all the historic buildings.

She went so slowly, in consequence, that though she

reached the church at last, she missed Louise by several minutes. Her first thoughts on seeing the chapel were quite different from Louise's. She thought how lucky Flora was, to have come from such a historical family. She thought how pretty the little figure on the tomb looked, what a great sculptor must have made it. And then she bent to read the lines written on the marble beneath the sleeping figure, only to find that they were all in Latin. Piloo's Latin was not good enough yet for her to be able to translate them. Nor could she read the French or Italian lines written on two other sides of the tomb. But on the fourth side, at last, she found the lines in English. "I was not in safety, neither had I rest and the trouble came." Oh how true, how wise, thought Piloo, tears starting to her eyes. It was just the kind of thing Mummyji and her grandmother in Calcutta might have said. But then, on the front of the pedestal, she found another inscription. Reading it made her tears fall in earnest.

"To Penelope, only child of Sir Brooke Boothby and Dame Susannah Boothby, born April 11th, 1785; died March 13th, 1791. She was in form and intellect most exquisite. The unfortunate parents ventured their all on this frail bark, and the wreck was total."

"The wreck was total," murmured Piloo to herself, even more overcome by the beauty and the sadness of the words than by the beauty and sadness of the sculptured figure. Tears dropping onto her scarf, she repeated over and over, "The unfortunate parents ventured their all . . . and the wreck was total." Oh if only Mummyji could see it. If only . . .

But she did not know, of course, how close Mrs. Bannerjee actually was to seeing it. She did not guess that Mrs. Bannerjee, and Aunt Jo also, were already halfway up the M1 highway in the Bannerjee family Volvo, and that they would be here in this church, at Penelope's marble tomb, not so very much later.

As for Flora, from the beginning of the day till it ended she did not know who she was, Flora or Penelope. She remembered everything; and nothing. On the one hand, Ashbourne was not a place she'd ever known or been in—the streets, the names on every shop front, were new to her. On the other hand, every way she turned she found something that was familiar. It was not just that so many of the buildings, the tiled roofs, the leaning gables were familiar. The men shouting and running, the crowd ebbing to and fro were familiar also. Even in the years Penelope had not been allowed out of the Hall to see the football, she'd heard the shouting, the roars of encouragement from the streets outside. There were almost three miles between the two bridges set for the goals, at either end of the town. She remembered how, as the fortunes of the game swayed this way and that, the sound of it would fade into the distance one way, turn, come back, then fade away into the distance in the other, "uppards and downards" of the Henmore Brook.

The Henmore Brook led from the fish ponds and was the first thing that, as Flora, she recognized. But the fields beyond, that used to be part of her father's private park, were now full of townspeople. A striped marquee had been erected in the middle. As for the fish ponds, she saw three ducks silhouetted across the bridge where one fish pond joined the other, but when she knelt on the bridge gazing down into the water, she saw no sign of any fish. Some cracker crumbs she found in her pocket attracted only ducks when she scattered them. And she had to get to her feet in a hurry because three young men rushed past, clutching cans of lager, and nearly knocked her into the water.

Flora reached the striped marquee just as a man mounted a small dais beside it, carrying a ball much bigger than a football, fatter than a rugby ball, and more misshapen than either. Having made a short speech of which she heard not one word, he started the Ash Wednesday game just as Penelope's father, Brooke Boothby, had started it, throwing the ball down into the crowd of excited men. The roar went up; the game began. The men and boys of the town, now as then, turned into mad creatures. Two hundred years ago Penelope's father had hoisted Penelope up so she could see the contest better. Flora, however, had seen enough to satisfy her that even in two hundred years, the football had not changed. Turning her back on the players, she set out to look for the other places she'd come to find—Penelope's places.

She headed for Ashbourne Hall first, of course, not bothering to consult Louise's map. She didn't need a map, she thought, as she crossed the hump bridge over the Henmore Brook. The memorial gardens she encountered, the road she had to cross, did not put her off. Though she had not expected to see such gardens, such a road, she found herself, shortly, in a street called Cockayne Avenue before what remained of Ashbourne Hall.

Only half the original Hall was standing. What was left proclaimed itself to be the public library. A crude extension had been added to one side. It did not look, though, as if it had ever been a very big or very grand house, the way that Flora remembered. It was made of dirty reddish brick, and the only aspect of it she recognized for sure was the big bay window at the front. Yet even that wasn't much bigger than any such window in an ordinary terraced house. And when Flora peered inside, expecting books in a library, she saw only a jumble of broken furniture and bare floors.

Where Doctor Darwin's carriage had stood on a sweep of gravel, where little dog Tray had met his death, a road now ran, within a few yards of the window. On the far side of it, in place of the lawn and the gate into the park, were the memorial gardens with their small conical bandstands and their big lych-gate. There were trees in the garden certainly, but none were big enough to have dated from Penelope's time.

The light was very bad now. Standing by the bow window, Flora looked beyond the gardens, across the meadow, the fish ponds, to where the low hills swelled on the far side of the valley. They'd been bare in those days. Now they were covered with houses. But in that light, at least until the yellow street lamps began pricking on here and there, she could not see the buildings. By half closing her eyes, she could even forget the road, the memorial gardens. She could imagine, almost, that she was seeing the same view as Penelope saw all those years ago. Indeed in that moment she *was* Penelope once more, seeing it all, then and now, tears trickling down her cheeks. But for whom was she weeping? For herself, Flora, of course; for Flora's mother, Flora's father. At the same time she was weeping for Penelope; for Penelope's father and mother; for all of them, for the dead and for the living.

She set off again, walking very quietly and sadly. Once she'd emerged from Cockayne Avenue, into the street that led up to the Market Place, she hardly heeded where she was going. She did not need to. It was a walk Penelope had done a hundred times before. Though the shops were not the same as the old days; though the streets were full, roaring with the football one minute, almost empty the next; though the road was macadam now, not cobbled, it was still familiar. Only the smell of an Indian restaurant, the Rajah Tandoori, pulled her out of the trance she walked in. For how could the smell of curry from an Indian restaurant fit with her being, walking, going, as Penelope to Ashbourne church? Under the Green Man sign, she went—the inn was closed now, shuttered and gloomy she saw, shocked—along past the great stone buildings of what was once an ancient grammar school into the churchyard.

Louise and Piloo had already come and gone. But the bent gray woman was polishing brass tablets in a corner, the verger busying himself in the vestry. Piloo had not noticed either of them. Nor had they noticed her. Nor did they see Flora, creeping in like a little ghost, making her way, unerringly, to what she had come for.

The white marble tomb was everything that she'd

expected. It was surprising how little feeling it aroused in her, what faint shadow of a headache. Unlike Piloo, Flora did not circle it reading the inscriptions; though she did take in, vaguely, that they were not all in one language. She did not even spend much time looking at the figure on the tomb. Instead, cautiously, she reached out a hand to stroke it, marveling at the different textures she encountered. The muslin of the cloth, the velvet of the sash, the rose-petal skin of the child's cheeks were all perceptible to her touch, though cold. Yawning, exhausted, her headache advancing, what Flora felt, chiefly, was a desire to lie down. Battered it seemed to her between one soul and another, between one time and another, she wanted to close her head, her eyes against either. To sleep the sleep of the very dead.

Penelope took up the whole stone mattress. But though there was scarcely room for another alongside, Flora was so thin, she did, somehow, manage to fit herself onto and around the marble image of her other self. They lay together at peace, like twins. If anyone had looked closely they would have seen, clutched in Flora's hand, a walnut shell; if they had opened that up they would have seen a child's tooth—two teeth. Whose teeth, who can tell? There were two bodies here. One warm, breathing, wearing a gray school skirt and gray school coat. One cold, marble, in a muslin dress. Outside and inside the marble tomb both slept—the sleep of the living; the sleep of the dead.

But it was not the verger who discovered them lying there together. The bent gray woman arrived first. Advancing toward the tomb, duster in one hand, tin of brass polish in the other, she could not believe the twin life, twin death, she saw there. Not only the stone head, the stone hair, of the marble twin; the straggling dark hair, the beaky nose, the long lashes of the living twin, were all too familiar. And yet how could they be, the woman thought wearily, discontentedly; how could they?

Chapter Twenty-five

"There were two of them, you see, Geeta. I never told Flora about that. Her mother hadn't. Pen hadn't wanted Flora to know she had a twin born dead, she thought it might upset her. But I did wonder, Geeta. I wondered if I should tell her. I wondered if it had anything to do with all this business; and if she'd known about it, might that have helped put her head straight? What do you think?" Aunt Jo appealed to her friend, as they drove along the quite narrow and often winding road between Derby and Ashbourne.

"I think you should do what your heart tells you, Josephine," Mrs. Bannerjee said.

"The trouble is, Geeta, I never know what it's telling me in all this," Aunt Jo said. She had rushed home that day on her lunch break to find the note left her by Louise. There and then she'd rung Mrs. Bannerjee. There and then Mrs. Bannerjee had come around in her Volvo. By the time Piloo phoned she and Aunt Jo had been driving along the North Circular Road already, on their way to M1 highway and Ashbourne.

"You are also thinking Flora's grandmother may live there still in Ashbourne, Josephine," Mrs. Bannerjee said. "And I'm sure you think once Flora sees such a smart lady, descended from a lord, she will not want to stay with you any longer. The same way I worry sometimes that Piloo will not know if she is Indian or English. In India, this running away business would not have come about, Josephine. Piloo is changing in England."

"She's growing up, Geeta, that's all it is. And perhaps we both worry a bit too much," Aunt Jo said. But she fell silent, then. They both fell silent, for they were approaching Ashbourne; only to find they couldn't enter the town with a car today, they had to park some way off.

"Trust Flora to come here today, of all days," said Aunt Jo, as she and Mrs. Bannerjee set out to walk to the church. Because of Penelope's tomb, that was the best place to start looking for Flora and the others, she'd thought. Off in the distance the football match raged; once or twice it sounded as though it was drawing nearer—Mrs. Bannerjee, to Aunt Jo's relief, didn't say anything about quaint English customs. It was getting toward dusk now. Figures loomed in the dim light. Men shouted. Both women began complaining about the distance they were having to walk. But at last they too arrived at St. Oswald's Church and went in to look for the Boothby chapel.

The first sight of it augmented Aunt Jo's fears that such past grandeur might all too easily go to Flora's head. But only for a moment. Flora was no longer sharing marble Penelope's bed. They did not find her. But as they turned away from the chapel, they heard the sound of running footsteps on the stone floor of the nave, and heard voices calling, "Mum!" "Mummyji!" The next moment Piloo and Louise had flung themselves on their mothers, amazed to see them, ashamed, yet half sobbing, half laughing with relief.

"It's all right," panted Louise. "We lost Flora but then we found her. A woman call Mrs. Jebb is looking after her, giving her tea; she's very tired."

"However did you get here?" Piloo cried. "When did you come?"

And then both began describing at once how they had met each other in the street, and then gone back to the church to look for Flora, arriving there just as Mrs. Jebb led the dazed, sleepy Flora out from the big stone porch. Mrs. Jebb lived by the church, it seemed; she helped out the verger. They had given her their telephone numbers; she had been calling their homes, or trying to, but there'd been no reply. As soon as they'd looked out of Mrs. Jebb's window, though, and seen their mothers going into the church, they knew why there hadn't been any reply.

By the time they walked back across the churchyard it was almost dark. The windows of the low stone house for which they were heading were golden with light. It had an arched porch like that of the church, but much lower and narrower. It did not look like a grand house, Jo noted. Inside the porch, the door was open; from it, too, light spilled out. But against the light, blocking it, stood a woman, a very thin, rather bent woman. Though Jo could not yet see her very well, she took it for granted—the name was enough, let alone the place—that this was Pen's mother.

How clearly she remembered the words Pen used to describe her mother. "A fat white woman," repeated Jo to herself, bemusedly. "A fat white woman whom nobody loves."

For though this must be Pen's mother, she wasn't fat. Yet it was true Pen hadn't loved her, or claimed that she had not. She had run away from her, hadn't she? But then what? thought Aunt Jo. Mrs. Bannerjee gave her hand a squeeze now as if she just knew what she was thinking. What about Flora? Would she come to love her grandmother? Or at least would she want to claim all the things her grandmother might offer? Jo thought of the tombs of Flora's ancestors in the Boothby Chapel and gave a small sigh.

But if this was her grandmother, Flora herself was not quite ready to take it in. Her grandmother did not seem wholly ready to acknowledge *her*, either. She asked Jo a great many questions. At the same time, she sat them all down in a kitchen so clean and bare it did not look as if it had ever been used to cook a meal, and plied them with as many cups of tea as they wanted and a small plate of Ashbourne gingerbread. Flora took two pieces of gingerbread, Jo noted, in some relief. She began to look less ghostlike than in a long time. For Flora *had* looked ghostlike, Jo realized. But she still looked thin, much *too* thin, Jo thought. Seeing Louise's eyes on the last piece of gingerbread, she lifted the plate and urged it instead on her adopted daughter.

Louise noted that Mrs. Jebb hardly took her eyes off Flora, yet never looked her directly in the face. Not only did Mrs. Jebb speak like the queen, she spoke to Aunt Jo and Mrs. Bannerjee as if she herself was the queen, Louise thought. Aunt Jo spoke to Mrs. Jebb in the polite way she talked to customers in the dry-cleaning shop; not at all the way she spoke to Mrs. Bannerjee, let alone to herself and Flora.

Once Mrs. Jebb went out of the room for a moment. And while she was gone, Piloo mentioned Penelope's tomb. Mrs. Jebb arrived back in time to hear her. "She was my ancestress," she said with pride. "I was called after her, like many other girls in our family. Before I married, I was, myself, a Penelope Boothby."

"So I am called Penelope, after her," said Flora in a small voice. Jo eyed her anxiously. She need not have been anxious. Flora was smiling at her grandmother for the first time. While her grandmother, almost looking her in the face at last, was almost smiling back.

She said, "I had a cabinet, once, belonging to Penelope, or said to belong to Penelope. It was an apprentice's piece, the kind an apprentice made, decorated with different kinds of ornament, to show what he could do. I kept buttons in it till Pen was old enough, then I gave it to her. Pen took it away with her when she went. It always has belonged to the youngest Penelope in the family, ever since the first one died."

Flora was not smiling now, she was grinning broadly.

"It belongs to the youngest Penelope *now*," she said. "It belongs to me. And I've still got all the buttons; everything," she said.

Putting her hand in her pocket, she felt the walnut shell, the one with the two baby teeth inside, nestling in their bed of faded green velvet. Her mother's teeth? Penelope's? It didn't matter. They were all dead and gone, weren't they? But she, Flora, wasn't dead and gone. And the apprentice's cabinet belonged to her, no less than her Penelope memory did, no less than her Flora memory. All of it now was part of herself. And one day, she thought, she, too, might have a daughter called Penelope. One day she might hand over the cabinet—and the buttons—and the baby teeth—to her.

It seemed quite clear to Flora now why she'd had Penelope living in her head all those years. Why she had known whose reincarnation she was. Penelope must have wanted me to know I was part of her family, as well as part of Aunt Jo's, she thought. And now I know. And I know I've got a grandmother, too, and I know where my real mum lived, and I know Penelope, the real Penelope, the first one. She would always feel sad, she thought, because Penelope had died so very young. But from now on, when she felt sad for that Penelope, she would not feel so sad for herself.

For she, Flora, wasn't Penelope, either in the eighteenth century or now. Penelope was only her second name, after all; she herself was twentieth-century Flora Worth. A girl who, though she had a grandmother in Ashbourne and ancestors lying in Ashbourne's Church, lived in Cardew Road, Hammersmith, London W6, with her Aunt Jo and her Uncle Frank. Who had a sister called

Louise and a brother named Alan, and a best friend from India called Piloo Bannerjee. She was not, she never had been, except in her head sometimes, Penelope Boothby.

That Penelope was truly dead and gone. Flora knows who she is now. She has a grandmother in Ashbourne she sees every now and then. But she still lives in Hammersmith with Uncle Frank and Aunt Jo and her cousin Louise. The only thing that's changed is that they no longer share the house with an aged and bad-tempered tabby cat.

It had been a survivor, that cat for sure. It had eaten its fill all its life and never been eaten. But age catches up even with survivors in the end. Uncle Frank had found it lying dead, stiff as a board, one morning in the backyard at Cardew Road. In its place the Worth family are now proud owners of a small white dog that they got at the Battersea Dog's Home the very next day. They call it Little Dog Tray.